Mr.
SEPTEMBER

Michele Dunaway

Dedication

For Robert L. Brown and all my former students who always inspire me

Chapter One

Ten, no, twelve rogue pirates surrounded her, the hot, humid air one of the reasons for her flushed skin, the men surrounding her the other. She trembled, for there was one in the midst who stood out over the others, who captured her full attention, held a magical power. He was strong. Dashing. A cad. He'd sidetracked her mission, yet as an illicit thrill stole over her, she wanted him to swoop in, scoop her up, and carry her away, help her escape from all this. His lips would fall on hers, taking her to never imagined heights . . .

Taylor Krebs blinked. Focused. Cleared her head, fading the Walter Mitty fantasy world she created, one she'd gleaned from reading bestselling Lalita Crane's latest historical romance novel. Last night Taylor had turned the pages until three a.m., a foolish choice in hindsight, as she'd had to be awake, dressed, and at the hotel by seven.

Now midafternoon, she was tired, hot, and—finally— almost finished with the job she hoped would ignite her career.

She had to get her head out of the clouds, although fantasy was almost always better than reality. Case in point, she was surrounded by twelve of St. Louis's sexiest bachelors and it was fast becoming her worst nightmare. She would much rather read about being surrounded by gorgeous guys, and hey, in her fantasy, maybe one of them could help her with the applied project due for her master's degree, the other task constantly taking up brain space.

She sighed, doubting very much that any of the sexy guys in front of her could help. And she needed the master's degree, for if she couldn't make it as a full-time photographer, a degree meant she could get a job teaching at the college level. As her mom kept harping, "You need a fallback plan, dear."

As it was, Taylor was so far behind on getting her project approved that entering it in the college's annual juried photo contest, the one with a thousand-dollar cash prize, would take a miracle.

"No, no. He needs a more seductive smile." Virginia Barker Edwards, calendar committee chair, clapped her hands until the poor man complied. "Much better," she called.

Taylor took the last shots and let the grateful man escape. She stifled a yawn.

Where was a rogue pirate when you needed one?

She made an adjustment to the camera, readying it for the next frame. At first, being chosen to photograph the Sexy Public Servants of St. Louis calendar sounded delicious. Who knew that St. Louis had such a bumper crop of handsome men?

There was Mr. December—cop Jack Donovan—in his Santa hat and low-rise jeans; Mr. January—park department's Blaine Johnson—in hat, tails, and tuxedo pants that fit like a glove; Mr. July—former Navy Seal turned SLFD marine rescue, Brad Silverman—wearing a pair of swim trunks and a smile; Mr. April—assistant District Attorney Liam Rogers—the only male wearing a shirt, although the partially unbuttoned white oxford had the same effect as if he was posing without it. Some of the female onlookers had actually swooned.

But for Taylor, it had been Mr. September—Joe Marino—who'd turned her insides into gooey marshmallow. She hadn't really paid much attention to the sexy firefighter. Not at first. Mr. Tall, Dark, Dangerous, and Brooding was so not her type. She liked them shorter. Blonder. Safer. More like ADA Liam Rogers, although the ADA hadn't made her heart race, hadn't made her do a double take like Joe Marino had.

Why was it she dated shorter, blonder men when heroes like the long-haired Duncan MacGregor from Crane's *Burning for the Rogue Pirate* kept Taylor reading until the wee hours, way past what was sensible?

She frowned as she swapped out the dead battery, using a backup one she'd forgotten to charge fully and prayed it would hold. She had one more month to photograph—September.

Her initial heated reaction to Joe had happened right before taking the group shots, when she'd peered through the viewfinder and zoomed in on Mr. September's eyes. Blue melded with light gray and a hint of green, forming a color that defied description. Which being without words kind of pissed her off, especially since she prided herself on description—it was part of being a photographer.

Worse, as if sensing her perusal, he'd winked. She'd zoomed out, caught, feeling as if Joe somehow knew what she was doing. *Impossible*. Still, her insides turned to oatmeal-like mush, and an indeterminable moment passed before her erratic heart slowed.

For Mr. September's portraits, Joe wore only his boots, turnout pants, suspenders, and coat—and a cheeky grin that well-intentioned mothers warned her about. Before Taylor had started Joe's individual shots, his second blatant wink had sent raw heat scorching straight down to curling toes clad in black and white striped high-top Converse.

Her tennis shoes were a concession to being on her feet all day, a downside to being a photographer. Camera settings adjusted, she was ready. Joe stood in the middle of the dance floor, in front of the bright green background. After the long day, his earlier cheekiness had vanished. She couldn't blame him.

"How much longer?" His impatient tone indicated his tolerance was wearing thin.

"Not too much. Just a few minutes more," Taylor replied, grateful the other months were complete. Because of Virginia's endless directions, each shoot had run over allotted time, and the men had ended up waiting around.

"Only a few more shots, I promise." She took them.

"There. All done."

"I want his coat adjusted," the calendar committee chair called out as Joe began to move. He checked himself mid-step, turned back.

"Well, maybe we'll need a *few* more," Taylor amended wryly as Joe scowled, those full, dark brows knitting together.

However, his surly frown was lost on Virginia Edwards Barker, the calendar chairwoman and the one who had everyone dancing to her tune. This was her pet project, and perfect silver hair remained frozen in place as her head tilted while she studied Joe over hot pink designer reading glasses. Her lips puckered. "He needs to show more chest. Definitely more chest."

The six or seven inches already exposed had sent Taylor's imagination into overdrive. The curly hair on Joe's chest matched the thick layers atop his head, and those glossy untamed raven waves kissed the edges of his turnout coat collar—bad boy, rock star hair that he wore better than her favorite lead guitarist.

"Taylor! Stat! Time is money. Let's not delay the poor man further," Virginia called.

The loud series of claps she added jolted Taylor to attention, and her face flamed. Betty White's younger doppelganger had awarded Taylor the assignment, so Taylor did Virginia's bidding. *No* wasn't an option.

Her fledging photography business desperately needed this break and the subsequent exposure the calendar would bring. Her bank account, drained from undergraduate and graduate school loans, needed the cash jolt.

So she trotted dutifully out onto the brown parquet, the white soles of her Converse making nary a squeak. Joe waited in the last pose: right knee bent, boot planted on a wooden crate, hands on hips. She reached for the worn mustard-colored edges of his turnout gear and pushed the sections of the heavy fire retardant material toward his sides. Her fingertips grazed rock hard abs covered with those tempting silky strands and her breath hitched, causing her to emit a tiny hiccup.

Twinkling blue—no, gray—no, blue eyes drilled into her. "Want some help?" Full, kissable lips inched upward, amusement clearly evident.

He was enjoying this!

Sensing her hesitation, he covered her trembling hands with his and, with his touch branding her unsteady, shaking fingers, he eased the coat off his shoulders so that more of his perfectly sculpted torso showed. He moved her right hand to his bare chest, and Taylor's mouth dried as her fingers resisted the urge to palm with abandon. She bit back the next threatening hiccup—her often-uncontrollable nervous reaction—and tugged her hands free from his firm grip.

Laughter lined those wicked eyes. "Like that? That work for you?"

Oh Lordy. *He* definitely worked for her, and having turned into a silly, childish puddle, she could only nod because her normally loud voice had vanished. Being she stood five foot five, he towered over her by at least a foot, maybe more. He was tall, lean, ripped. With a body carved from real life, he shamed all the sex-on-a-stick men gracing the covers of the Lalita Crane historicals she devoured.

Forget hot, he was smoking—a man's man—the irresistible kind that gave women extremely erotic dreams.

"That should work," Taylor finally managed, praying no one watching had heard her exhaled whoosh of edgy breath. She and Joe stood toe-to-toe—every one of Taylor's nerve endings on high alert. She wasn't a naïve teenager, but she'd never been so physically aware of a man— especially one like Joe. Her brain screamed *run*, but her feet clung to the ground. Her hands desired to fully feel his chest, test the texture for herself, curl her fingers into the silk.

"What about his hair?" Virginia called. "Don't you think we should fix that? He has some hat head."

Joe reached up, dragged his hand through his hair.

"No, that's not what I want," Virginia returned, her lips puckered in clear disapproval. She held her hands up and wiggled her fingers in the air. "Muss it up. Make it sexier. Do you know what I mean?"

Unfortunately, Taylor did. She inhaled patience and composure and called back, "Yes, I've got it."

A sexy black eyebrow arched, curiosity evident. Joe's lips moved, capturing her dormant libido's complete attention. "You do?"

Taylor blew out a deep breath, which was followed by a hiccup. She winced. "Stand still."

She rose on tiptoes, her plain red T-shirt inching up to reveal a sliver of pale stomach. Threading both hands into Joe's hair, she pushed the wayward locks off his forehead. "Sorry about this."

The thick strands caressed her fingers—no grease or residual gooey product here. *Just shampoo and natural waves.* Her skin heated like an inferno. His breath hitched as she pushed his hair up and over, patting any loose pieces to make them stay. "There."

"Am I good?"

Uhhh, he was more than good.

His eyes had darkened to blue steel, held a hint of something. . . . "Didn't know we knew each other so well. Not that I minded. Was it good for you? If not, I could make it good."

"I said I was sorry." Taylor gave another embarrassing hiccup.

His deep, suggestive voice caressed over her in a smooth wave. His lips twitched. "Don't be sorry. *I'm* not. Who knew modeling could be so . . . hands on."

"Uh . . ." Her tongue tied into knots. In her favorite novel, the hero would have kissed her now. He'd lower his mouth to hers and . . .

"That's better." Virginia's voice broke the intimacy, reminding Taylor that she stood in a rented ballroom, in clear view of the others, making unprofessional googly eyes with her subject.

"I'm much happier," Virginia called out. "Very sexy Joe. Just what we're looking for. Now get the shots, Taylor.

Didn't he say he had to leave? Why are we still keeping the man waiting?"

"Yes, let's get this done," Joe replied. Aware of their audience, his grin widened and he lowered full lips to whisper in Taylor's ear. "But you just let me know if you need anything. I'm happy to oblige. Maybe we should explore what else those expert fingers of yours can do. I'm a very hands-on kind of guy. Comes with the job description."

The seductive way his words rolled off his tongue made no secret that he meant the double entendre. "Yep, more than happy to help you."

As Taylor scurried back to the safety of her camera, his low chuckle burned her ears. *No way did she need more of him!*

Joe Marino was bad news. The kind who ran into danger instead of safely away. If one glance, or one hand on that hard chest, had turned her into a heated wreck—and she prided herself on being a woman who was never, ever, out of control—what would touching him more do? He'd shattered her precarious control with mere words.

"He reminds me of that werewolf in *True Blood*," her friend Marci whispered as Taylor refocused her camera. The black Canon SLR was like a security blanket, and she moved it in front of her right eye.

One thing was certain—the camera loved Mr. September. The lens captured all his hard angles, accentuating them and making them even more chiseled. Taylor swallowed the next hiccup, which came out as a faint, mouse-like squeak.

"You know, the actor. What's his name? He also did that firefighter dance in *Magic Mike*," Marci continued.

A movie Taylor had sadly missed. But she knew the HBO show. Had seen every episode with her girls' viewing group, read all the Sookie Sackhouse books. "Joe Manganiello."

Marci snapped her fingers. "Yeah, that's him. See what I mean?"

Eye to the viewfinder, Taylor could perceive the resemblance Marci claimed—both men had the same dark hair and super-cut body—but really, the generalities were where the likeness ended. The Joe in front of her was clean-shaven. She could probably crack an egg on that sculpted jawline. He wasn't as broad in the shoulders. He stood taller. His hair was longer, wavier. And his deep, sexy voice definitely hadn't been the same. "He might even be hotter," Marci said.

Marci was dead on, one hundred percent correct, but Taylor ignored answering her flirtatious friend, who'd only volunteered to assist on the photo shoot so she could hang out with twelve, hunky single men.

Taylor, being too poor to hire an assistant, had welcomed the help, even though that meant Marci flitting from guy to guy, her search for Mr. Right as fickle as the number of times she changed shoes per day. Marci had shed her earlier four-inch heels for a sensible pair of Sperry's. Despite Taylor's Converse, her feet screamed for a warm footbath.

Mr. September planted his hands on his hips and widened his stance as Taylor pressed the shutter, catching his poses. "Now if you could just move your helmet . . ."

"Here?" He dropped it directly in front of his crotch, and she flushed.

Virginia let loose a giggle. "Oh Joe! You are so bad." Narrowing her gaze, Taylor frowned. She'd sworn some of the women in Virginia's entourage had swooned.

"Under your arm will be fine," Taylor returned briskly as his wicked grin split into devilish laughter before he complied. She pressed the shutter and the camera clicked rapid-fire. She issued a few more orders, and Joe executed the subsequent positions without complaint or comment, much to her relief. The man was danger personified.

"Okay, we're finished," Taylor called. "Unless you have anything else?"

Virginia shook her head. She appeared a bit flushed. "I'm satisfied. And it's hot in here."

"Great. I always make sure a woman is pleased before I leave." Joe strode from the dance floor and headed their way.

"He's going to be a favorite," Marci observed.

"He will," Taylor agreed. She had well over a hundred fifty photos—surely Virginia would find something she liked. Taylor wiped a drop of moisture from her forehead. The hotel's air conditioning had failed miserably with keeping up with the unseasonably warm June day. The temperature outside was ninety-nine; it had to be at least eighty inside. The large fans designed to give the men the windblown look had provided some relief, but not nearly enough. She'd clipped her long auburn hair up off her neck and into a loose knot, but that hadn't done much. Her unsecured natural curls had frizzed into a hellacious halo.

Joe reached the set of chairs. He shed his coat, slid the suspenders down. Six-pack abs rippled as he pulled on a navy T-shirt embossed with the fire department logo. Then he sat down and pulled off the boots. Rising, he slid the turnout pants down, revealing the blue work pants he wore underneath. She knew he had to have been uncomfortably hot wearing all his gear. But he hadn't complained once, unlike a few others. After realizing that Virginia hadn't planned on providing food and drink, Taylor had sent Marci to the nearest convenience store for two dozen cold bottles of water, a Styrofoam cooler, and a bag of ice. Her charge cards already bleeding, what was one more unplanned expense?

As the group began to disperse, Taylor grabbed one of the last bottles. Unlike those TV modeling shows with multiple computer monitors on tables, Taylor's reality was a used light kit bought off Craigslist, the green screen, and her camera. She'd work on her MacBook later and process the images. Shot against green, she'd easily be able to Photoshop the men onto the various St. Louis backdrop photos she'd taken previously. Then, once done, she'd bring the disk to Virginia.

"Tuesday, my office," Virginia reminded Taylor of the upcoming deadline as she and her entourage made to leave.

"Ten a.m.," Taylor confirmed. Today was Wednesday,

so she had almost a week to get the images ready. As she had double shifts at Presley's Friday and Saturday and thousands of photos to process, she'd need every spare minute. The hairs on the back of her neck rose as a rich, sexy voice said, "Can I see?"

Taylor turned. Joe stood there, towering over her in the T-shirt that fit like skin. He gestured at the camera, the small Maltese cross tattoo on the inside of his wrist clearly visible. She'd kept the tattoo out of view during the shoot. Virginia's orders—and what Virginia wanted, Virginia got.

"There are hundreds of images . . ."

"I don't want to see all of them. Just the last few will be fine."

"No one else saw theirs . . ."

That sexy irresistible grin slid into place, and Mr. September turned into Mr. State the Obvious. "I'm not like everyone else."

No, he certainly wasn't. No one else made her heart skip or her face flame. Now in the clothes he'd wear around the firehouse while waiting for a call, Joe shouldn't be so intimidating. Shouldn't be so alluring. Shouldn't be calling to something deep inside, something primitive she'd buried two years ago, something too dangerous to allow out.

"Besides, you owe me. You had your hands in my hair and on my chest. Surely that gives me some leeway, a little extra."

Ooh boy. "Fine."

The devilish grin widened. "See how easy that was?"

As Marci went to roll up the backdrop and put away

the light kit, Taylor turned on the camera's preview mode and scrolled through the last few images. Joe leaned over her left shoulder and watched as she did. "That's good work."

She paused, surprised. "Thanks. You're not going to make a comment about how I had a good subject to work with?"

"That goes without saying." His now trademark smile came and vanished. He shrugged. "Seriously, though, I can tell you've got talent. I hate being photographed. I never look good in them."

Add lying to his list of talents. She scoffed. "Then why did you do this?"

He frowned. "Because I had no choice."

Ha. Hardly. Somehow she couldn't quite believe him. "Everyone has a choice."

He opened his mouth, checked whatever he'd been about to say, and instead returned to the wide sexy grin found in all the photos. "Perhaps I just wanted to meet you. Get to know you."

"Oh please. You're being a cad. Be serious." Taylor threw a hand over her mouth, realizing she'd sounded like the heroine in the book she'd clearly needed to put down last night. How embarrassing.

Hands went on hips. Eyebrows arched. "A cad? Where does that word come from anyway?"

From a romance novel. Face flaming, she turned the camera off, watched the screen go dark. The backup battery had done its job of allowing her to finish the shoot. She made a show of putting her Canon into the camera bag, but Joe didn't take the hint. "I'm sure you have other places to be."

"You called me a cad. That's a low blow. I have to defend my honor."

"Are you serious? I was joking. I'm sorry if I offended you."

He shook his head, that lovely hair caressing his jawbone. Her fingers longed to touch the thick strands again, run her fingers through them, and draw them away from his face. Clearly, the book's steamy love scene was wiggled into her subconscious.

"Humor me. You had your hands on my chest—and good hands, by the way."

"Part of my job."

"Why'd you become a photographer?"

"Why'd you become a firefighter?" she returned.

"Not for the reason you think, and do you always answer a question with a question?"

Her chin jutted forward. She was intrigued but tired. "Why? Does it annoy you?"

Deep laughter erupted, and shoving his hands into his back pockets, he disregarded the bad habit that sent most men she met running for the hills. "I like challenges; I don't scare easily."

Not expecting that answer, her next inhale went down wrong, and she coughed.

His forehead creased. "You okay? Need me to bang on your back?"

The thought of him touching her made all her nerve endings go haywire again. "I'm good. No need." She made show of touching the base of her collarbone. At least the hiccups had stopped. "Hate when that happens."

The easy grin returned. "You seem to have some breathing issues today. I'm a certified paramedic. I'm trained in mouth-to-mouth. Let me know if you require that."

The thought of his lips touching hers caused her next breath to whoosh out. No man had made her react so viscerally. She would take charge. Put him in his place. "I'm fine. I really need to pack up. So if we're finished . . ."

"Actually, I have another question for you."

The directness of his answer made her stare, curious. "Oh? What is it?" Was he about to ask her out?

"I like the work you do, and today I saw how patient and kind you are with your subjects. I'm looking for photographer to help me with a pet project. Interested?"

Damn. For a millisecond disappointment filled her and she wiped the back of her right hand on her forehead, the lack of decent air conditioning starting to get to her, or maybe it was simply his dynamic proximity. Of course he didn't want her—just her skills. But, she'd hoped. Anticipated. *Get it together*, she chided herself. He hadn't even really been flirting—just more annoying, right?—and she certainly couldn't turn down business. "I'm willing to listen."

"Perfect. Card?"

His entire demeanor turned serious, and she remained

frozen, the change so abrupt she was certain her head would be spinning if not attached. "Yes. Hold on." She dug into the front of her camera bag, took out a tiny piece of heather gray cardstock.

He plucked the business card from her fingertips, studied the words, and tucked it into a front pocket, the movement creating a crease in the pants near his. . . . She jerked her gaze away. "Great. I'll call you in a day or two. That work?"

"Uh. Um. Yes." She forced herself to be professional.

"Good. Can't wait to talk then." He thrust his hand forward, and unprepared for the gesture, she shook it awkwardly. Like when he'd covered her hands earlier, a sizzle fused her fingers to his, forcing her to pull away quickly. All day he'd had her off her game. She was drawn to him but wasn't sure she liked him. After the huge ordeal of her breakup with Owen, she avoided anything or anyone that made her feel out of control, which was how she felt since his first wink. But she needed work. "Talk to you soon."

With that, Joe picked up his gear and strode to the exit. Taylor stared, stupefied, unable to rip away her attention as she tracked his progress. She was no match for this man, this gorgeous chameleon who could charm his way into getting whatever he wanted. As for exactly what he wanted, he'd led her one way and then switched directions so fast she hadn't been able to keep up. Did he really need a photographer? But why would he pretend otherwise?

"He is so hot," Marci said, approaching with the gear. Her enthusiasm bubbled. "He took your card. Did he ask you out? God, I wish he'd have asked me. Are you going to go? You should. Especially since he's single and you haven't had a real date in ages. Not since Owen. It wasn't your fault he was such a jerk and . . ."

As Marci rambled on, Taylor pressed her water bottle to her forehead. She was getting a massive headache. Time to get some real food and into some actual air conditioning—stat. As for Joe Marino, she dismissed him from her mind, although it took more effort than she'd expected. No matter how much her body liked him, she was a girl who'd learned the hard way to follow her head and not her heart. And her head said to stay far away from Joe. Even if he did make her mushy. And hot.

***

"Look! Mr. Sexy's back!"

"September," Joe returned, ignoring the teasing whistles as he strode through the open bay doors into the firehouse, gear in hand. "Get it right."

"Get what right? That you're not sexy?" Reid shot back. "We already wondered what they saw in you."

"Good one," Chris, another member of Joe's squad, called out from where he was performing inventory. "You might want to quit while you're ahead, lieutenant."

"Ha-ha," Joe replied. He balanced the gear on one arm, grabbed the clipboard from Reid with the other, looked the contents over, and initialed on the line where required. Reid retrieved the board. "I can see you all at least got some work done while I was gone."

"What did you think, we'd just sit around playing video games?" Kyle, the third squad member said. "Well, maybe Parker did. Why'd you sub him again?"

Joe countered with the obvious. "Because a truck can't go out unless it has four guys?"

"What about me? Did I hear someone say my name?" Parker asked, ambling over. A full-time lieutenant from Station 26, Joe's brother-in-law had covered the portion of Joe's shift so he could do the shoot. Amazingly, the department had even sprung for the overtime. Somewhere up the chain of command, someone had decided that sexy firefighters made for good PR.

"They were just saying how much they like working with you," Joe fibbed. "Any calls?"

"A car accident," Parker said. "Guy hit a light pole. Pretty quiet today."

"Don't say that!" Kyle winced and slapped a hand over his temple. "You jinxed us!"

"Yeah, now we'll get called out nonstop for the rest of our shift," Chris groaned. "Thanks a lot Parker."

Parker grinned. "Doing my part to help. Pretty boring over here. I like it when there's some action."

"Yeah, well, we don't mind boring," Chris said. "Lots to do. In fact, we need to clean—"

The second Chris said the word "clean," Parker started moving. "Nope, my subbing's done. Done my good deed for the day."

Joe rolled his eyes. "Yeah, for the overtime."

"Well, there is that. I'm supporting your sister and niece, you know. But, you've got a good crew or I'd never agree to set foot over here. See you guys later. See you Sunday, Joe."

"What's Sunday? Why aren't we invited?" Reid called.

The gear weighed heavy in Joe's arms. "What, you all want to come to my nephew Ben's birthday party? It starts at noon. Picnic area near the Living World. I'm sure he'll appreciate all the extra presents."

"Will there be a bounce house?" Chris asked. "I might be there if there's a bounce house."

"Although be sure to secure it so it doesn't fly away," Kyle warned. "Remember that video? Don't want to take that call."

"No bounce house," Joe said. "We're in Forest Park so we can barbeque and visit the zoo."

"Aww, that's sweet," Chris teased.

Reid grinned. "I like the zoo. And your mom's a good cook. Is your sister Elaina going to be there?"

"You stay away from Elaina." Joe scowled, for his sister dating Reid was the last thing he needed. The youngest on Joe's squad, Reid had gone to high school with Elaina, graduating two years ahead of her and her twin brother Peter. There'd been enough drama when Susie had started dating Parker. Then again, look how well that had turned out. They were perfect together, giving Joe hope that someday he might find that special someone who could see past his own flaws. Being oldest, at least his siblings had provided his parents with the requisite grandchildren, so that pressure was off.

"All I want from Elaina is more brownies," Reid replied innocently, but Joe didn't believe him. "Remember the last batch she brought? The iced ones? Those were delicious."

"Yeah, she makes good desserts," Chris threw out. "My wife hates baking. When's your sister dropping by again?"

"Enough!" Joe called a halt. He loved his crew as much as his family, but they had work to do. Stationed in a firehouse built in the 1960s, there was always something needing repair. He'd start whacking down his to-do list after grabbing a sandwich. The shoot had lasted the entire morning, and then two hours into the afternoon. Photographed last, he'd missed lunch. He figured there'd be food—but clearly the organizer had forgotten that. At least the photographer had sent her assistant out for bottled water.

He had to admit, twelve guys and one bossy organizer plus her entourage were overwhelming. But the photographer had handled the shock with aplomb. She'd also had hazel eyes—the kind you could drown in. He was a sucker for eyes—he always noticed those first. Hers had been magnetic, pulling his gaze time and time again to her perky round face, where he'd seen full, kissable lips. She had a body that simply called out to a man . . .

As part of him stirred to life, he checked those

dangerous thoughts, settling for a safe *Well, she'd been quite easy to look at*, which had made the shoot far more bearable than he'd expected. She'd also been good at her job. He'd meant it when he'd said she'd captured him pretty well.

Today was a win-win. He'd found who he'd been looking for, for while he liked to tinker with his SLR camera, he was a never going to be anything but an amateur. He needed her help, for he'd tried to take the portraits himself for the project he'd mentioned to her. However, he'd quickly discovered his eye wasn't as good as he'd hoped. His technical ability was even worse. He couldn't capture his subjects correctly, and they deserved the best. He needed professional help.

He'd found her interesting; his body had shot to attention after her long, firm fingers had pushed his coat aside—well that didn't mean anything. Basic biology. Besides, he didn't have time for a relationship and he never did casual. Ever. Women couldn't handle him or his baggage, and baggage was something he had in spades.

While he needed Taylor, it was for her photography skills, nothing more. No matter how much he liked her lips and wondered how they'd taste. No matter how even some light flirtation had brought to the surface that dormant feeling he was somehow missing out by curtailing his love life.

He began stowing his gear, pausing when the loud two-tone buzzer created a familiar burst of adrenaline. The speaker voice called out for Squad 3 and Truck 5 for a three-alarm fire. His crew scrambled into motion, tugging on gear over their clothes before climbing into assigned places. As the senior squad officer, he sat sho-gun, securing himself as Reid threw the vehicle into drive. The location came up on the GPS screen.

"So much for boring," Chris said over the headphones.

"I'm going to kill Parker the next time I see him," Kyle said. "He jinxed us."

They fell silent, mentally readying themselves for the firefight. A three-alarm blaze meant multiple engine and ladder companies would be at the scene, and as today was excessively hot, crews would be able to work only so long before the battalion chief ordered them to take a mandatory cooling break.

As they raced through the streets of South St. Louis to the warehouse fire, an image of Taylor flashed through Joe's mind before he pushed it away. His day had never been boring, not with her in the picture. He'd talk to her soon enough, for once he set his mind on something, he didn't stop until he got his way. He'd set Taylor in his sights, and getting her to say yes to his proposal shouldn't be too hard. He'd use the full Marino charm. She wouldn't be able to resist.

Chapter Two

Presley's on the Landing was the kind of bar that changed personalities depending on the time of day. From the moment the doors opened at eleven a.m., Presley's served up an assortment of pretty good burgers and wedge-cut fries in an industrial, warehouse décor with dark wood tables and exposed brick walls. With waitresses wearing shorts, respectable T-shirts, and bright, Kelly green aprons, the restaurant was somewhere patrons could bring kids or hold an important business lunch.

Around nine p.m., however, Presley's performed an about-face. A beefy bouncer sat on a stool at the front door checking IDs. Inside, live music pounded at deafening levels, belted out by local rock bands all trying to get signed. After nine, revelers could still find food, but waitresses in tighter, lower-cut T-shirts and shorter shorts concentrated on delivering copious amounts of alcohol to twenty-somethings desiring to let loose, drink, dance, and hook up.

Taylor had worked three p.m. to three a.m. on Friday, and as she arrived at work at a quarter past three Saturday—late—she forced herself to shake off the cobwebs. Last night had been rough. Even though the bar kicked the last drinkers out at three, she'd cleaned until well past four. Too keyed up to sleep, she'd crawled into bed and read *Burning for the Rogue Pirate* until five, when the first hints of sunrise tested her room-darkening blinds.

She'd planned on catching five hours of solid shut-eye before getting some photo work done, so she'd set her alarm for ten. All week, she'd been processing and manipulating images in between making cold calls to drum up some business and serving burgers. She still had a lot of work left to do on Virginia's calendar pics. But instead of waking, she'd accidently turned off the alarm instead of hitting snooze, allowing her to sleep until almost two-thirty. When she'd woken up and realized the time, she'd took the world's fastest shower, got dressed, and left.

Luckily Presley's was relatively quiet—the weekend lunch crowd having departed and the early dinner crowd not yet arrived—so she hadn't been missed. She clocked in, greeted one of the other servers with whom she was friendly. "Hey Beth, how are you?"

"Did you forget?" Beth frowned at Taylor like she had grown horns, and Taylor shivered.

She'd been scatterbrained lately, but aside from her Presley's shift, today's calendar had been clear. "Forget what? I know I'm late. Is John mad? We weren't supposed to wear a specific shirt, were we?"

"No nothing like that, so no worries. He's not here anyway. He ran out for a minute. I just can't believe you forgot."

A little wrinkle formed between Taylor's eyebrows. "My life's been a bit crazy trying to get all this work done."

"No excuses. Today's the day for the Station 31 charity. You should see these guys!"

The wrinkle deepened. "What are you talking about?"

"The firefighters. They're working as servers. Donating their tips to charity. The lunch shift left about a half hour ago and ooh la la."

Taylor groaned as she remembered John had said something about the event weeks ago, before she'd promptly forgotten all about it. "That's tonight?"

Beth nodded. "Yes. The next group will be here at four. Lunch was testosterone overload." Beth waved her left hand in front of her face. Gold flashed. "I tell you, if I wasn't happily married . . ."

"I'm sure Todd's grateful for that fact," Taylor teased.

Beth put a hand seductively on her hip. "You bet he is. Every night. But I can still look at some mighty fine men, especially when they are our esteemed city firefighters. It's our civic duty to ogle, right?"

"Sure." Taylor laughed. Beth and Todd had been married about three months and Taylor had photographed their wedding. "Let me check what tables I have."

"And which firefighter," Beth added. "Should be a packed house tonight. Hunky eye candy while we do the real work. Although they can carry a tray, if you'd like."

The way the event worked, a corporate sponsor covered tips so the servers didn't lose out, which Taylor appreciated as she had a school loan payment due.

She also had rent due and needed a new telephoto lens. While Virginia had paid a small retainer, Taylor had spent that money on supplies. The balance—the part she'd make as profit—would come when Taylor delivered the job. If she had a good shift, like she'd had last night, she could muddle through financially until then—for no way was she taking her mother up on the offer to move home. Better times had to be ahead, didn't they?

"Speaking of grad school, how's your final project going?"

"You mean my nonexistent project? The one I've so far failed to find?"

"That bad, huh?" Beth asked.

"I've submitted at least thirteen ideas, and my professor keeps turning them down. Who would have thought a master's in Media Communication would be so difficult? It's like he hates photography."

"But that's what you love."

"Yeah, but so far I'm batting zero. I have to find something, and fast. I thought I'd be well on my way, yet here I am. I'm too late to even enter the juried show. I could have used that money toward a deposit on a storefront. Now I'm just trying to graduate."

"Don't be so hard on yourself. You'll figure something out and finish on time. You're a great photographer. I have faith in you."

"You might be the only one. Even my mother's given up. She keeps asking when I'm moving home. Hey Libby. Where am I at?"

"You've got this section," Libby, the hostess, pointed to the laminated layout of restaurant tables. Taylor nodded, pleased. She liked working the back room, as it was furthest from the band and the dance floor. While she'd still be busy, it meant less elbowing her way through the craziness. The people who sat in the back usually talked more, drank longer, and ordered food, all adding up to a better tip.

"Let's get ourselves set up," Beth said.

She and Taylor took seats in an empty booth and began rolling knives and forks inside paper napkins before sealing the lots with adhesive paper strips. Taylor had quite the stack of flatware by the time a prickle of awareness crept up her spine. Then she heard her manager John's voice . . . and a bunch of others.

The firemen were here.

"Gather around, everyone," John's voice boomed. Standing with him were ten firefighters wearing jeans and neon pink shirts. The union logo was on the left sleeve, and a two-inch outline of a ribbon adorned the space over the heart. The back read "Station 31 Pink Out." Clearly the chosen charity had something to do with breast cancer, which made sense as St. Louis's Race for the Cure took place in June.

John began his pep talk. "Tonight we're going to raise some funds." Taylor half listened. She stood on the outside of the circle, looking around at everyone's backside until a familiar head of wavy black hair had caught her attention. Elastic secured his hair at the nape of his neck, creating a one-inch poof. Trepidation stole over her.

With all the firehouses in the city, this couldn't be Mr. September's unit.

But as John finished his monologue, the firefighter pivoted, and that part blue, part gray and green gaze locked onto hers. Taylor's stomach dropped. Joe. His wolf grin widened. "I'll serve with her," he told John, taking a step Taylor's way.

Her manager shrugged. "Works for me. Taylor, this is your guy." Then John began pairing everyone else up.

"Did you hear that?" Joe asked as he approached Taylor. Hypnotic eyes she hadn't been able to forget twinkled, and her gaze fixed on his full lips. "It seems that I'm your guy."

Taylor's best defense was always offense, so she puckered her lips as if she'd sucked on one of the lemons from the garnish dish on the bar. "Ha. Funny. You don't have what it takes be my guy."

His grin never wavered and his deep voice went even lower. "Remember, I like challenges."

Her body reacted, drawn to his like a magnet. *Must . . . regain . . . control.*

"Well, you failed the challenge of dialing a phone." Taylor added a toss of her head, and her ponytail swished. "Whatever you needed to talk to me about, it clearly wasn't important."

He put his hand on his chest, acting astonished.

"What, were you waiting with bated breath?"

"Hell no," she retorted, irritated at how easily he'd already gotten her riled and gone crawling under her skin. So much for control. And, darn him, she had thought of him often, wondered what he'd wanted. Clearly it—she?—hadn't been important. "I'm a busy person, and I assumed you'd call as you seemed so insistent. So whatever your project is, it'll have to wait. I'm booked."

She wasn't, but pride demanded she pretend.

He glanced around, absorbed in the surroundings. "So this is your day job."

"Don't say it as if I'm a failure."

Those blue-green-grays drilled into her, and his tone sharpened. "Did you hear me say that?"

No, but like everyone else, he'd probably thought it. "I am a photographer," Taylor emphasized. "But this helps pay the bills."

"I didn't insinuate anything." He thrust his hands into front jeans pockets, making his arms tense. Muscles bulged.

"We need to get started." She made her way over to the rolled flatware, indicated he should grab some. "These need to be placed on all the tables." She pointed. "Those are our tables. So put one in front of every chair."

"Will do." He began placing silverware. "And I didn't mean any offense. I saw your pictures. You're not a failure. Hardly."

"Well, my work doesn't yet pay all the bills. It's a competitive field. You missed a table."

"Oh." He went back. "So how old are you?"

Her chin jutted slightly. "Twenty-six."

"I've got eight years on you. You have plenty of time to make it." He'd finished the silverware. "That means you can take more risks."

"Not if I want to eat. Speaking of eating . . ." Taylor grabbed a menu off a serving station and handed it to him. "You might want to look the menu over. Tonight's specials are written on that photocopied insert. The chef bought too much tilapia, so we need to push that."

He opened the menu, glanced over everything. "Fine. Tilapia it is." He handed the menu back.

"You don't need to study it more?"

"Been here before. And really, it's not much different from any other place. Just locally owned and known for the night life."

"True," she conceded. The hostess came by, leading a family of four. "Looks like we have our first table."

He rubbed his hands together. "Excellent.'

She held out the order pad. "You'll need this. We don't have to memorize things here."

"Even better." Their fingers touched as he took the pad of paper, the pink T-shirt accentuating his tanned skin. Real men really did wear pink. Joe wore it even better.

From the bios she had on all the calendar men, she knew he was thirty-four, had been involved in some aspect of becoming a firefighter since he'd done Explorers in high school.

Perhaps that's why he strode up to their first table with

complete confidence. "Hi, I'm Joe from Station 31 and I'll be your server, along with Taylor here. I'm a bit out of my element, so please be patient. What can I get you to drink? A portion of everything goes to charity, so I hope you're hungry."

The couple laughed, as did their teenage kids. Taylor stood behind, ready to assist, but she wasn't needed. Joe wrote down the family's drink order and handed it to her. The firefighters wouldn't do the computer entry or enter the kitchen. Presley's staff would do that part.

Their tables filled up quickly, which thankfully kept their conversation to the bare necessities of serving food. That left her time to observe. Like he'd been on the day of the photo shoot, Joe was incredibly charming. His gorgeous smile and teasing style had people buying extra drinks. He sold multiple tilapia specials. He got customers to eat dessert, even when they insisted they were too full. She and Joe had a steady crowd all night—every server did.

"So, how's your hunk doing?" Beth asked as they stood next to the computer touch screens while the media interviewed several of the firefighters.

"He's not my hunk. And he's doing fine."

Their manager, John, caught the last part and paused on his way to the kitchen. "Fine? So far Joe's our top seller. The man is a money-making machine. Heck, I'd hire him if he wanted a job."

"Yes, well . . . I only meant . . ." Taylor gave up. Joe could clearly do no wrong. The monitor flashed. "My food's ready."

She escaped into the kitchen. When she returned, Joe stood waiting and easily took the heavy tray from her. He served a table of six while the busboy cleaned one of the four-tops in their section. Libby soon appeared carrying menus, leading the way for two men and two women. Recognizing one of the men, Taylor froze and subconsciously receded from view.

Owen.

Two years wasn't enough time. No amount of escapist reading had let her forget. Bad memories rushed through open floodwalls and, fingers trembling, she made a beeline for the wait station. "I need you to take table fifteen," she told Beth. "It's my ex."

"Oh." Beth's eyes widened, understanding even though Taylor had never shared the full story. "Of course. I'll take it. Uh-oh."

Taylor turned to see Joe already greeting them. "Just don't go over there," Beth said. "I'll do it."

Joe took the order, glanced around and frowned. Locating Taylor, he walked over with the drink order. "Why'd you disappear?"

"Because you're doing great on your own," she said, which wasn't an outright lie. "I think you've got it from here. There's only an hour left. How about you handle that table by yourself?"

"Yeah, I can, but I thought you were supposed to—"

"What did they order?" Beth interrupted, taking the pad out of his hands. "I'll enter it for you."

"A bucket of beer and hot wings," Joe told her.

"Great." Beth's fingers tapped on the touch screen. "Done."

"So what's the problem?" Joe asked, turning to Taylor. "Something's changed. I'm not moving until you tell me what's wrong."

He'd already reinforced how much he liked challenges, and Taylor didn't need him prying even further into her life. She doled out a crumb, enough information to get him to leave her along. "It's that last table. The hot wings one. See the guy?"

Joe craned his neck. "There are two."

"One's my ex."

He scowled. "Which? The blond?"

He'd guessed correctly, but she said, "It doesn't matter. Listen, just do me a favor. I'm going to switch tables with Beth for a few. Hang back here."

Beth smiled at Joe, who didn't seem pleased with the new arrangement. "Fine. If that's what you want. It's clear it must not have ended well."

Taylor's lips thinned. The breakup had been an absolute nightmare. "Which is why it's best I'm not seen."

"Well, I'd never have pictured you being the run-from-your-problems type."

He studied her while Taylor folded her arms defensively. "Seriously? Do you have to be so offensive?"

"See, there's the backbone I've come to know. And again with the questions. Seriously, I'm not trying to offend you. If you'd just tell me the whole story, maybe I could help. That's what I do. Help."

She bristled. "My personal life is none of your business and I do not need a knight in shining armor. Just do me this favor and we'll get through tonight, go our separate ways. One favor. That's all I ask."

Those all-knowing blue-gray-greens that defied description saw straight through her as she withered under his superior scrutiny. "Look, there were mitigating circumstances, and it was two years ago, but for the sake of everyone, including his date, Beth's on point for that table."

Beth had already moved off to serve one of her tables. Joe folded his arms, which unintentionally emphasized his broad chest. "Fine, but the fact remains you and I still need to talk. So be forewarned, I'm planning on cashing in on the favor you just offered."

His words created an illicit thrill that combined with momentary panic. "We do not need to talk."

Ignoring her, he shook his head, grabbed the bucket of beer the bartender was handing over, and walked away.

Taylor fumed as she watched him go. He didn't know the whole story—the nightmare that had been her life or the restraining order that had expired a year ago. She didn't scare easily. But in Owen's case, playing it safe was always better than being sorry. Who knew how he'd react to seeing her?

She managed to avoid Owen during the hour it took his party to eat, pay, and leave. During that time, she'd hardly talked to Joe, which was probably safer as well. The fundraising event was nearly over, and soon the over-twenty-one crowd would take over. That meant the firefighters would leave.

She picked up the leather bill folder off a vacated table and carried it to the computer station. The table had left a twenty-five percent tip. "So, do you have a few minutes to talk?" Joe asked, appearing at her side.

Every time he came near her, she jumped. She forced her heart to slow, struggled for calm. "I'm really busy right now. It'll only get worse."

"When do you get off?"

He was persistent, she had to give him that. Dog-with-bone determined. She told him the truth, something he could easily find out if he asked her boss. "I'm off at three."

He frowned. "Three?"

She entered the tip into the computer. "Yes. Three. I'm closing. This is the Landing, you know."

"I thought *my* hours were crazy. I guess it's better than the East Side." He passed over another bill sleeve. "So can you spare a few minutes now? I'd like to talk before I go."

"I'm—" The phone in her apron pocket vibrated. Only three people ever called this late, and none meant good news. She swiped unlock, put the phone to one ear and a finger in the other in an attempt to block out excess noise. "This is Taylor."

"Hi Taylor." It was Linda, a nurse at in the maternity ward of a local hospital. Taylor got ready for the bad news. "Triplets. One arrived stillborn. Are you available?"

Taylor's grip tightened on the phone as her heart broke. "Yes. I'll be right there. About twenty minutes."

"Thank you." She could hear the relief in Linda's voice. "I'll let the family know."

Taylor ended the call by hitting the power button. Luckily her manager walked by. "John, I've got to go. Emergency."

John's face fell. "Another one?"

Taylor nodded. She'd worked for John for three years now, and he understood why she had to leave and what she needed to go do. He had three kids of his own. "I know I'm leaving you short. I'll be back as soon as I can."

He waved her onward. "Go. We'll handle it."

"Great." Taylor took off her apron.

Deep creases formed on Joe's sexy forehead. His jaw ticked. "Hey, I thought we were going to talk. Why are you leaving?"

Her thoughts already on the family she was about to meet, Taylor said, "I have an emergency. I don't have time to lose. I've got to go."

"I'm an emergency expert. Let me help." His whole demeanor changed. Standing before her was a man who dealt with multiple crises on a daily basis. His voice contained a quiet authority that soothed and calmed.

Shaken by seeing Owen earlier and the news she'd just received, she wavered. "No, you can't, but thanks for offering."

Joe planted his hands on his hips, took charge. "Don't be stubborn. Your hands are trembling. Your heart rate is up. I'll come with you. We can talk on the way. Kill two birds with one stone."

Taylor stared at Joe. How dare he. Yet knowing the

strength she'd need over the next hour, and after seeing Owen, she didn't have any more energy to expend fighting with him.

"Let me help, Taylor. Whatever it is, I can handle it." His assurance swayed her; he clearly exhibited leadership in a crisis. And she did have to come back here anyway, so it wasn't like he couldn't retrieve his car. Maybe some company—even his—might be welcome, considering the circumstances. "Fine. You can ride with me. Let me clock out. And we'll go."

***

As Taylor disappeared into the kitchen, Joe motioned for Reid's attention. His entire crew had been assigned this particular charity shift, and Joe had been surprised when he'd seen Taylor. He'd had no clue she wasn't a full-time photographer. "Something came up and I'm going to cut out early," he told Reid. If Reid thought the request odd, he rolled with it, made a joke.

"Yeah, I saw the hot redhead. I'd cut out early too."

Joe scowled. "Can you just take over without the crass commentary? She was the photographer from the calendar shoot. She's not a hook-up."

Reid shrugged. "Hey sorry. I'll keep the guys in check. We're just serving food. How hard can it be? I got this."

"Great. Thanks. See you." Having just finished a forty-eight-hour shift, Joe and his crew were off for the next ninety-six hours. Taylor reappeared, walking so fast that

Joe quickened his step to catch up.

He followed her outside, around the building to a small private parking lot. She pressed the remote and the lights flashed on a four-door, late-model, black Chevy Cobalt as the doors unlocked. He folded his body into the passenger seat, reached down, and eased the seat back. He'd barely fastened his seat belt before she'd backed out of the parking space.

"Where are we going?" he asked as she zipped her car through the Landing traffic.

"Hospital." Her knuckles tightened on the wheel as she shot through a yellow light. He put his hand on the top of the doorframe for balance.

"Is it your family?"

"No. Not family." She whipped around a curve and he braced himself. While he was used to racing through city streets, it was in a multi-ton fire truck with lights flashing and sirens screeching. "Do you always drive this fast?"

"When I need to."

He gripped tight again. "How many tickets have you gotten for reckless driving?"

"None," she retorted, braking as the light turned red. He jerked forward, then back. He noted this was one of St. Louis City's new red-light camera intersections,, or he suspected she'd have gone right through. "I'm a very good driver."

"That's open to interpretation, but seriously—"

"You didn't have to come," she retorted.

"And miss being in a road rally? Nah. So . . ." he prompted. "What's going on? How can I help?"

The light changed, and she sped up the entrance ramp to Highway 64. "I'm needed at the hospital. A set of triplets. I'm going to take photos for the family."

He knew the kind—the ones taken right after birth. He had five wallet-sizes—one for each of his nieces and nephews. "So you drop everything for those photos?"

She floored the gas and wove past a slower car. "No. That's not what I do."

"Then you've really lost me."

"Set of triplets. One didn't make it. That's why I'm going. I take *those* photos."

"Oh." He hadn't expected that answer. Hadn't realized parents would request a photographer to take pictures of their deceased infant. The fact that she'd dropped everything raised her up another notch.

Lost to his thoughts, an awkward silence settled. She exited at Kingshighway, made her way into the parking garage, and swiped in. The gate arm lifted. "You don't have to come. It's not pleasant, and I'm sure you don't understand. But even though the baby's no longer alive, it helps the mother to hold her child, and I'm there so that the parents have some sort of tangible memory, a photograph of what their baby looked like. Not every parent wants my service or wants to remember. But many do. They want a picture so that their child never is forgotten. And time is of the essence."

"I see," he said, although he could tell she probably didn't believe him. "Let me guess. Few people get what you do."

He'd surprised her with his insight. "Maybe you *do*

understand. Most look horrified. Find me freakish."

"I won't. I'm here to help."

"Be sure to keep quiet," she told him as she parked. "That's rule number one. If you can't do that, then I need you to stay in the lobby."

He scowled. "I'm a professional. I can handle this."

She assessed him, deciding if he passed muster and if she should trust him. "I guess death isn't new to you, is it?"

Freed from constraints, his wavy dark locks swished as he shook his head. "I've seen far more death than I'd like."

She faced him and her expression softened. "Yes, you probably have."

A muscle in his jaw twitched. "Often we're the first ones on the scene. Car accidents. Heroin overdoses. Fires. We do everything the paramedics do, except transport in the ambulance."

"So you really are a firefighter paramedic?"

That made him chuckle. "I wasn't making that up. We all are. It's required. I really can do resuscitation. If you need it."

Taylor's fingers tightened on the steering wheel as she pictured the sexy man in the passenger seat putting his lips on hers. Her face heated, and she was glad she was inside a darkened car, illuminated only by the lights of the parking garage. She cut the engine and pressed the trunk release. The hatchback popped open. "Okay, let's go."

She rounded the car, removed her camera bag. The slam of the back closing echoed through the partially empty garage. She strode toward the elevators, and they took the pedestrian bridge into the hospital and the elevator up to labor and delivery.

"Taylor." Linda stood as Taylor and Joe approached the nurse's station. Relief erased Linda's exhausted expression. "Glad you're here."

"Wouldn't be anywhere else. This is Joe Marino. Firefighter. Okay that he's tagged along? I'm showing him the ropes."

"We've moved the two girls to the Children's NICU." Linda pronounced the name for the newborn intensive care unit as "Nick-U". "The mother is in recovery. The boy was stillborn. I'll let the family know you're here."

Taylor knew that many hospitals had labor and delivery rooms that changed into maternity rooms—a one-room-for-the-duration concept. However, here mothers were moved to a mother-baby unit, where mothers and babies spent as much time as possible together in the same room. Linda disappeared into a room down the hall and came out a few minutes later. "They're ready for you."

Joe hovered behind Taylor as they entered the room, which had been somewhat tidied. The mother sat in the bed, a wrapped bundle in her arms. She looked like hell: brown hair a scraggly mess, sorrowful eyes puffy with tears. Her husband stood at the window, his gaze elsewhere. He turned as they entered.

"This is Teddy," the mother said as Taylor stepped next to the bed. Mom adjusted the blanket, and Taylor and Joe could see the baby's face. Teddy looked like a pale, motionless doll. "There were three heartbeats just days ago," she said. "I don't know what happened."

Joe froze. How many times had he heard those words during a call? *I don't know what happened.*

Far too many to count.

From experience, Joe knew Teddy's parents would repeat that phrase over and over. No matter how many times Teddy's mother was reassured, she'd never believe that it wasn't her fault. For the rest of her days, she would question what she could have done, if anything, to prevent this moment.

Taylor adjusted the blanket, moving it lower, and as sorrow shot through him, Joe had to briefly avert his eyes.

"Thank you for letting me share this with you," Taylor said, impressing Joe with her gentle, empathetic bedside manner. "I know it's hard, and I'm going to make sure you have all the photos you need. He's a beautiful boy."

"My Teddy," his mother said, softly touching his motionless cheek. "When they're older, I want his sisters to know what he looked like. I want them to remember he loved them."

"Of course they will. I'll make certain of that."

Joe took a steadying breath and glanced at the wall. He'd seen a lot, but the sensitivity of the scene in front of him tugged at his soul. Yet Taylor clearly knew exactly what to do. No tears threatened to fall from her eyes—despite his assertion of professionalism, his were somewhat wet. Her voice soothed as she issued simple instructions. The camera clicked as the shutter opened and closed, a gentle, comforting rhythm as Taylor captured the son who would never age.

The entire photo shoot took under ten minutes, but Joe felt like he was in a hazy dream, as if time had stopped. He was seeing Taylor in a totally new light, a perspective that solidified his decision that she was perfect for the photography project that was his life-long penance.

As Taylor finished, time began again and reality intruded. Joe moved closer to the door, giving Taylor space as she squeezed the mother's hand, telling her she'd email the family access to an online download within forty-eight hours. As they left the room, Linda held out a card that provided the family's contact information.

During the ride down the elevator and the walk across the pedestrian bridge, another silence fell. Joe had no words for what he'd just witnessed. Taylor was a hero in her own right, doing a difficult task because it needed to be done.

As Taylor set the camera bag in the trunk, he found his voice. "Can we go get a drink?"

She shut the hatch. "I need to get back to work."

He wasn't ready to leave her. "You can't spare a few more minutes?" His voice hitched. "Please. Break your plans. Dressel's is around the corner. I'll buy. It's the least I can do. Let me do something."

She must have heard the urgency—or was it agony or desperation or a combination of all three?—in his voice, for she surprised him by nodding. He saw her tremble as she opened the car door, looking at him across the roof. "Yeah, I think John can spare me a little longer. Get in. I could use that drink."

Chapter Three

Five minutes later, Taylor wedged her car into a tight spot on Euclid, just across the street from Dressel's Public House. Wanting to maintain some iota of control, she hadn't told Joe that he'd picked one of her favorite places or that it was one of the reasons she'd agreed.

One of her clearest memories of her father was when he'd brought her to dinner at Dressel's. Later, as an undergraduate at St. Louis University, she'd often returned to the pub once she'd turned twenty-one and could enjoy the libations. The other reason she'd agreed was because being with Joe made her tremble, and she hadn't felt any lingering interest in over two years. For tonight, she'd like to feel alive, to remember what it felt like to receive the attention of a beautiful man.

They walked the short distance through the comfortable June evening. They sat on the sidewalk deck, and although the hostess placed two menus down before departing, neither Joe nor Taylor reached for one. "Are you hungry?" he asked.

"A little," Taylor admitted, leaning back and trying to relax. She was admittedly extremely type A; her mom said she'd been tightly wound since birth. Owen had called her high strung and overreactive. She wondered why her ex had eaten at Presley's, why he'd even shown up there. Maybe he thought she didn't work there anymore. He'd always hated her job, claiming waitressing beneath her. Still, even after a year, it was a chancy move to eat there after their explosive fallout.

A server passed by, and Joe caught her attention. "Could I have two waters and the potato chips with rarebit?"

"Sure," she said, disappearing.

"That'll work to start," Taylor said. Her stomach rumbled, agreeing.

"I figured we could nibble first, see how hungry we are. Or where we were on time."

"Good call. Thank you." A waiter brought over two tumblers of iced water and introduced himself. "I'm Leo, your server. I've put your chip order in. What else can I get you?"

Taylor mustered the energy to smile at Leo, a young guy with a sleeve of tattoos. It wasn't his fault she was exhausted. "May I have a house Riesling?"

"Absolutely. And you?" He turned to Joe, who ordered an English-style brown porter produced by a local craft brewer. "Great choice. I'll be right back."

"The weather is perfect," Taylor said as Leo retreated.

She sipped the water, while watching a car drive down Euclid. The sky was full black; they sat beneath the streetlights.

"I wanted to tell you I'm sorry," Joe said.

"For what?" She unwrapped the flatware, put the napkin in her lap and the silverware on the metal table.

"You were right. I've been a jerk. Hell, probably been a real ass."

Taylor couldn't help herself. Her lips inched into a smile. "And you just realized this?"

"The questions return." He chuckled, amazingly not offended by her instant rebuke. "I'm sure I deserved that. Although you could simply be kind and accept my heartfelt apology."

The man had a way of getting under her skin, and his knees were far too close to hers.

"As long as you try not to do it again. An apology's only as good as the actions behind it. I learned that lesson the hard way."

"Well, I'm good for it. Scout's honor." Her lip puckered, and he laughed, a warm, rumble. "All the way to Eagle. I won't lie to you." He turned serious, drummed his fingers on the metal table. "I don't lie."

Their server returned, bringing Joe a draft beer that was a deep brown with a white-foam top. Joe sipped, and wiped his top lip where foam had dared to alight. Taylor swallowed, clutching her fingers in her lap.

"How is it?"

He motioned with his glass. "Excellent. Want to try?"

"I'm okay." In the soft, warm light he was even more handsome. Unclenching her hands, she reached for her wine and let the tarty Riesling roll over her tongue. She sighed, savored. "This hits the spot. Thanks for suggesting we come here. I honestly wasn't ready to go back. It takes a lot out of you, you know?"

"Actually, I do know, which is why I'm glad you could spare a few minutes. I'll admit I needed them." He drank, worked on finding the right words. "The baby. That's tough. I was amazed by what you did tonight. Your composure. I almost lost mine, and that never happens."

His admission surprised her. She leaned back. "Surely you've dealt with similar things."

"Yes." He moved the menu aside, settled deeper into his chair, the hot pink fabric molding to his torso. His leg stretched, coming closer to hers. "Yes." He hesitated, then chose to share. "I've seen plenty of things. But never like that, not during childbirth. She was at a hospital, not a fire or accident scene. It's the twenty-first century. We have advanced medicine. Childbirth is not supposed to be deadly."

"It happens more than you'd think."

"Tonight seemed personal for you." Lips wrapped around the glass edge. He was very perceptive. Owen had never understood, never wanted to. She watched Joe swallow.

"It is," she admitted, in the spirit of sharing. "Every time I do it, I hope it makes a difference. My sister lost her baby. Evelyn was twenty-six, my age now. Newlywed. Got pregnant on her honeymoon. Nine months later, about a week before her due date, she had these contractions and when she went into the hospital there was no heartbeat. The hospital had a woman who took photos, but she was out of town. So I stepped in. I don't even know how I managed to get any shots through my tears, but I did. Seeing my niece lying there so still. She wasn't red. Her skin was so bluish gray."

She reached for the water instead of wine, drinking as she remembered. Her hand trembled. "Claire. My niece Claire. And ever since, I just kept doing it. It's like I'm trying to bribe the universe for the next time Evelyn tries. Or for whenever I finally get ready to be a mom. Here I am a struggling photographer who waits tables to pay the rent because my main photo gig is performed pro bono. I would never charge those parents after what they've just been through."

"The universe will pay you back. You're building up good karma," Joe replied. His beer had lost some froth as he'd drank about a third.

She fiddled with the fork she didn't need. "I'm not sure I believe that anymore. It certainly hasn't so far. I'm even trying the graduate school route so I can go into teaching. There was this competition I was going to enter, but I couldn't get my professor to sign off on my project. I just keep hoping it'll get better."

"Well, you met me, didn't you?" He gave her that trademark grin, the one that she liked more and more the longer she sat with him.

She tilted her head. Considered. Refused to concede. "I'm not sure that's a convincing argument that good things are coming my way."

"I do." Joe spoke without a doubt in the world. "At some point fate's got to give, right? That you've paid whatever debt you think you owe and that life suddenly smiles on you? That you are on the right side of things for once?"

She drank more wine, letting the fuzzy feeling go to her head. She liked how her cheeks warmed. With food, the pleasant sensation would quickly fade, leaving her very sober, back to the reality of the night, and her life.

"I wouldn't say fate is working against me. I'm just not where I want to be. I had these visions of getting out of college, getting hired by a big New York City magazine, and seeing the world. Didn't happen and within two years I was back home." *And dating Owen.*

"But my life isn't bad," she continued. "Not when you like what you do, and I do love my photography. It just doesn't pay the bills so I'm late nights at Presley's. It's that or move home, and so far I've managed to say no to my mom's constant pressure to do that. What about you?"

A shadow passed over his face, or maybe the flicker was Leo bringing their homemade chips and cheese dip. He set them down, asked if they needed anything else and, when both shook their heads, left.

"Why'd you become a firefighter?" she asked, loading up her plate with chips and cheese. The rarebit was fabulous.

"It's in my blood," he said, putting chips on his plate. "My dad was one. My brother-in-law is one. My grandfather."

"You have a large family?"

She'd given him the opportunity he needed. "Yes. There are six of us kids. I'm the oldest. My sister Susie is a burn survivor. She's the one married to a firefighter. Not many people can see past her scars, but he could."

"I'm sorry."

He waved her comment aside, as if brushing away a mosquito that dared get through the perimeter. "It was a long time ago. She's why I'm so passionate about the book I'm doing for burn survivors."

He wiped the sweat off the glass. His leg had come into contact with hers; the denim rubbing against her bare calf. "See, I made my sister a promise, long ago. She's part of the Burns Recovered Support Group. The book will be portraits of burn survivors and their stories. A celebration of triumph. After what I saw tonight, I know you're the photographer I want."

"Oh." Taylor washed down the cheese-covered chips with more wine.

He drummed his fingers on the metal table. "It'll be a great opportunity, but we can't pay you anything. But the exposure will be great." He gave a harsh laugh. "You probably hear that a lot."

"A time or two." Taylor realized her wine was almost empty, so she drank the last sip. "I make tons of cold calls trying to drum up business and trying to get invitations to bid. It's how I landed the calendar project. A lot of blind luck and the fact I work cheap. They couldn't afford anyone else. I was the lowest bidder. But it paid off. So I get it. You had to ask."

"How much do you charge? Like, what was the price for the calendar shoot?"

Taylor named the figure. "And that includes all the postproduction work. That takes tons of time. I'm still Photoshopping the calendar-shoot pictures."

Joe shook his head. "I can't afford that. Neither can the group."

She could hear the disappointment in his voice. "I can help you find someone."

"I'd rather have you."

The words washed over her, making Taylor wish he meant them in another context. She'd connected with him on a level she didn't understand. Frankly, her attraction scared her. She'd let him climb into her car, taken him on tonight's emotional shoot. She'd never shared that experience with anyone. After what had happened with Owen, the fact she'd immediately trusted Joe spoke volumes.

Joe reached for a chip, dipped it in rarebit, and placed the cheesy morsel in his mouth. Perfect lips wrapped around the bite. He was temptation personified—she had the urge to see him open those blue-gray-greens on the pillow next to hers. And what would it be like to run her fingers through that luscious hair while she made love to him?

She hiccupped, so she took a deep breath then reached for her water. After a long drink, she calmed. Just one hiccup this time, not more. *Whew.* "You'll find the right photographer."

"I have. Your empathy makes you the right person for this project. I realized that when I saw you behind the lens during the calendar shoot. Now, after what I just saw, I'm positive. This book is going to get a lot of publicity. Would that help sway your decision?"

"So will the calendar," she pointed out.

He arched his eyebrows. "You can't use more?"

She wavered. "Of course I can, but . . ."

He pressed on, sensing her indecision. "Many of the participants are civic leaders. You'd be amazed at the list of who's who and you'd make some extremely valuable connections. One man is the leader of the St. Louis Film Commission. He works with every movie that's made in the bi-state area."

"Which haven't been a lot," Taylor felt compelled to point out.

"True." He popped another chip into his mouth. "But he was involved in *Gone Girl* when it filmed down in Cape. You have to start somewhere."

She sighed. "I've been trying to start somewhere since I graduated. Do you know how many unemployed photojournalists are out there?"

"More than there are jobs, which is why you need mine." They were making serious headway on the chips, and she reached for another. Chewed. Swallowed.

Considered what it was about him that made her throw caution to the wind and say yes.

He continued. "Look, I have an SLR that I play around with, usually when I'm out on a hike or climb, but there's no way I can do what you do. I've tried. Since your degree will let you teach, can I pay you to give me some lessons? You could help me take the portraits of my sister. I should be able to afford that. Do you take family portraits?"

"I take everything."

"So how much do you charge for that?"

The waiter brought her another glass of wine, one she hadn't ordered. She glanced at Joe. "Did you order this?"

He nodded. "You looked like you needed it. So? How much?"

The Riesling was ice cold and refreshing. "Well, there's the sitting fee based on the amount of time and the number of pictures I take. I include the images free via an online site as part of my services. You can download and take the files to Walgreens and print whatever you want yourself. The machine even lets you pick the sizes." After another sip of wine, she named some figures.

He didn't seem bothered by the costs, which were a fraction of the calendar shoot, so she relaxed and ate more chips. Finally he spoke. "That's doable, so how about I hire you to photograph my family? My mother's wanted all four generations in one big picture—not all of the grandchildren were at the last wedding and my grandparents are creeping up there. Since Mom's birthday is the beginning of July, I'll give her a family portrait sitting as a present. Will that work? I'll have to run the idea by her, but I'm positive she'll say yes."

Taylor opened her mouth, but as if sensing she might answer him with a question, he kept going. "Besides, my mother knows everyone. If she loves your photos, she'll drum up business for you all over the South Side. She's a human tornado. No problem she can't solve. So portraits and lessons. How can you say no?"

"With me needing cash, you know I can't." She shifted, aware she'd had her leg pressed next to his for a long time. "Only a fool turns down paid jobs. So. I'll give you a lesson and take your family portraits at the price I quoted."

He settled back in his chair. "Good. It's settled then. "

"I require fifty percent down."

That wicked grin returned, tugging at something deep inside her. "Not a problem. I'll call Mom tomorrow. See how simple that was? I've never met a problem I can't solve. It's why I like firefighting. It's man versus fire."

"I'm not a fire."

"No, but I'm hardwired to help. It's my nature, and this is mutually beneficial. Just think of all the time we get to spend together." He raised his beer glass, reached forward to tap it lightly against hers. "Cheers. I think this is a great plan."

She studied him over the rim. The wine had made her relaxed. Correction. Warm. Mellow. Slightly giddy. "We don't have a plan."

"No?" He tilted his head. Wrinkled his nose.

She shook her head. "No. We agreed, that's all. An agreement is not a plan. Plans are outlines. Details. To-do lists. I'm meticulous planner. Drives my mom nuts. She swears I can't be her child since she's such a free spirit."

He laughed. "So tell me how your plan works where I'm concerned."

Her brow creased. "Honestly, I don't know. I haven't figured it—you—out yet, or your real endgame."

"Well, I told you. My book. As for getting together so we can plan, I'm off for forty-eight more hours, so we'd have time to meet up."

"Must be nice."

"Not really, considering I only got about six hours sleep total over the forty eight hours I was on shift. Dealt with a three-alarm fire and a bunch of EMS calls. Every time we finished one, we went out again. Also, I had report after report to complete. I have to get those done before I leave. In between all that is the daily work that must be done."

"Yeah, I guess that would be hectic. I overslept today. I'd planned on getting more photos Photoshopped, but now I'll have to do them tomorrow."

"So your perfect plan went to hell."

She laughed. "As it so often does. Case in point, I'm here with you."

"Well, I'm glad you broke your plans." He directed the full force of his charming smile at her, making her toes tingle.

They polished off the last of their chips. He pointed at the empty basket. "Shall we order a pretzel? Or would you like something else?"

A pretzel sounded wonderful, and she wasn't ready to leave. Could she admit it? She was actually enjoying herself. "Let me call into work. Check on things first."

His eyes twinkled with mirth. "Good plan."

Taylor made the call, and John told her the place wasn't yet crowded now that the diners had cleaned out. "Just be back in about an hour," he told her.

Taylor hung up. Joe gazed expectantly. "Well?"

"The pretzel will be fine. I've got another hour." Especially since the bread would absorb the wine. Her face had heated with that wonderful wine numbness, meaning she definitely needed to sit longer before even thinking about driving. Besides, the evening and company had actually turned out better than expected. Joe wasn't exactly the jerk she'd thought he was earlier. Sure, he had rough edges, but he was a charmer. An unabashed flirt. He couldn't help himself, she decided. Like all the heroes in the escapist, delicious romance novels she loved, he just needed a good woman.

She must have already imbibed too much wine, for the thought that she could be that woman flickered across that wine. Leo popped by, Joe ordered, and Taylor sought safer ground.

"I can't imagine growing up with five siblings," she said, reaching for her water. Heck, she needed a long, sobering drink before she had him starring in tonight's dreams as well.

"The youngest is Elaina. She's twenty-five."

"A year younger. Almost my age."

"You'd probably get along. We're one big Italian family. You should see our get-togethers."

"Elaina's not the one was burned." Taylor worked to keep everyone straight. She'd never been this much of a lightweight.

Joe shook his head. "No, that's Susie. She's twenty-seven."

"How did it happen?"

His face clouded, as if the memory took him back to a bad place. "A grass fire that got out of control."

"How old was she?" Taylor sipped more water. "I'm sorry. I don't mean to pry, but you were the one who bought me that second glass of wine. I get chatty when I drink. Bad, annoying habit."

"It's okay. She was five. I was twelve. I couldn't save her from getting hurt." More of the dark ale he'd nursed all night passed his lips.

"I'm sorry. I shouldn't have pried."

"It's okay." He parroted. "Bad things happen to good people."

She thought of her father. Of Owen. Understood where Joe was coming from. A light breeze blew, and she reached up and removed her ponytail holder. Reddish curls cascaded around her shoulders, and she reached behind her neck and shook the strands to loosen them. Thankfully nothing had frizzed too badly. "So is your sister the real reason why you're a firefighter?"

"One of many," he admitted. "It's why this book is so important to me. Susie never felt beautiful. Growing up, people thought her freakish. All that burned skin. All those reconstructions, but it's never perfect again. People recoil. You can literally see them do it."

While Taylor had grown up with other children wondering why her father had never attended any school events, Taylor couldn't imagine what Susie had gone through. "I'm sorry."

"Then she met Parker and thank God he saw beyond the surface. They've been married for five years, and I'm godfather to their three-year-old daughter Winnie. I'm grateful he came into her life. She deserves to be happy."

"Yes, she does. We all do." Taylor recognized underlying guilt when she saw it. She'd had enough guilt herself over the last few years and could tell he had it in spades.

"Can I be blunt?" she asked. "You were just a child."

"That doesn't matter." Joe's fingers flexed hard against his glass.

"Yes, it does. When I was seven, before I lost him, my father gave me some good advice. He said you help everyone you can, and as long as you tried, as long as you did your best, that's what matters. It's why I take the photos. Why I keep fighting even when I'm down."

"It's not the same for me. You don't understand."

Maybe she didn't. She shook her head. "Perhaps not, and I shouldn't presume to try. But I do know that whatever it is, you can't blame yourself. So if you are, stop. There, my Dr. Phil for the day. Is he still even on?"

"No idea."

She pushed her empty wineglass aside. Her face flamed. "Whew. Forgive me. That was probably extremely rude of me. I overstepped. Now I'm the cad. It's an old fashioned word, but I rather like it, you know?"

The corner of Joe's lips inched upward. "It's okay."

She didn't believe him. She'd sounded like a fool. "You keep saying that."

"It's true. Remember? I don't lie."

She relaxed. "This wine must have gone to my head. Whatever you do, don't order me another one or I won't be able to drive. At some point I have to get back to work." The trees above rustled in the breeze. "Although I really don't want to. It's been a long time since I've sat out on a patio and drank wine. This is nice. Despite my bad manners."

His tempting hair swished with every shake of his head. "Don't sell yourself short. It's been refreshing, actually. Enlightening. Most women hide everything. Play games. You're blunt. You don't hold anything back. I like that. A lot."

She blushed again. He was good for her ego. "I wish other people did."

"Ah, now it's your turn not to be so hard on yourself."

A car moved slowly down the street, temporarily diverting her attention. She watched until the taillights disappeared. Leo placed on their table a Bavarian pretzel that was the size of a small loaf of bread. She leaned forward and tore off a huge chunk, all the way to the first knot. She placed it on her plate, tore it into tinier pieces, and dipped a morsel into the fresh cup of rarebit.

"I love this cheese," she gushed, putting the entire warm, gooey bite into her mouth. She chewed slowly, savoring the softness of bread melting in her mouth. She'd almost forgotten how enjoyable it was to sit with a man and just talk and enjoy great conversation. "I'm glad we decided to stay."

"Good. Me too."

Taylor took another bite, knowing that her guard slipping where he was concerned had nothing to do with the wine. She had to be sure not to be like all her favorite heroines who suddenly became blind to the hero's flaws. Hadn't that been how she'd overlooked all the problems with Owen? She'd refused to see the truth until too late. Hadn't she promised herself not to jump into fast forward with a guy ever again? Yet something about Joe made her want to toss caution to the wind.

"So tell me about your family." He held her gaze until she glanced away, her mind realizing that he'd gob smacked her. He was already deep under her skin, a guy who probably didn't like her except for her photography skills. She had to stay focused, not think about marrying the man five minutes after meeting him. "I told you about mine," he cajoled.

He had, and no question to lob back came to mind. "It's just me, Evelyn, and my mom. My dad died when I was eight. Navy test pilot."

"I'm sorry."

"It's okay. You told me about your sister. I have memories, like that advice I gave you, but as I've gotten older, I admit they've faded. I have to see pictures to really remember."

She toyed with the empty wineglass stem. The fact she'd had two glasses had to be the reason she was telling him all this, right? "But he died doing what he loved. There's something in that, I guess."

"Your mom never remarried?"

"She never will. She says one great love was enough and she's in a good place. She works at a perennial nursery and designs landscapes. She volunteers at the symphony. She's always busy. But Evelyn and I would love it if she found someone, but she's not even interested in looking."

"What about you? Do you believe in that one great love?"

She couldn't help herself. "Do you?"

"Ah, the questions return. . . . For a moment you were doing so well."

The wry grin returned as he shook his head in mock disbelief. Her fingers again itched to feel his hair. Wanted to see it cascade over him as he lowered himself over her. She waited while he tore off some remaining pretzel.

"Fine. I'll indulge you," Joe said. "Yes, I do believe in it. My parents are great role models. So, yes, I do want eventually want something like that. But as you complained about earlier, I'm nonstop busy. I never get around to calling anyone, and I'm not a nine-to-five guy, so it's hard to sustain a relationship. Things are always complicated." She noticed a hitch in the way he said those last three words.

"Complicated is my middle name," Taylor admitted. "And I could see how your schedule gets in the way. But you do get time off."

"Which I use to rock climb, box, to try to keep my house clean and train for marathons."

Her eyes widened. "Really? You box?"

His lips twitched. "Most people are impressed with the marathons."

"Tell me more about boxing. I'm looking for a project."

He frowned. "What do you mean?"

"I'm struggling to find an applied project for my master's degree. It's like a thesis, but instead of doing a written paper, I'm trying to come up with a photography project that has impact, that makes a difference. I need something my professor will agree with, and maybe, just maybe, will allow me to enter into the competition."

"Is money involved?"

"If I win, and I can't even enter unless my professor recommends me. Right now, I just want to get this degree done."

He again intertwined his legs between hers as he stretched out. "Well, perhaps you could do the Guns 'N Hoses competition. That's in November. I'm five and oh. I helped the firefighters claim victory last year."

"I can't wait until November. It has to done by the end of July. And what is guns and whatever?"

"Hoses. It's the police versus firefighters boxing match. All proceeds go to charity. The BackStoppers."

"Sorry, it's clearly very important to you, but I have no idea." She brightened. "I'll Google both of those."

"Do. The event is huge. Over seventeen thousand people attended."

"And you run too."

"Yes."

Which explained why he was so fit, other than staying in shape for work. The pink shirt showcased bulging biceps and hard pecs. He'd been pure temptation all night. "I'm not really into sports other than baseball or hockey," she admitted. "I can't afford to go much, but I'm what you call a see-it-for-free-on-TV fan. Presley's always carries the games. I loved when we won the Stanley Cup. And I went to the parade."

"Then you're a fan. That's what counts. So, I saw your ex. Anyone else in the picture?"

"No." Her fingers tightened around the edge of the metal table. "I'm glad he's moved on. I was shocked, that's all. It's a big city. I didn't think I'd run into him ever again."

"Well, the table seemed pretty tight. He was holding her hand."

"He's probably with her."

"Well, if you see him again, hopefully it shouldn't be a big deal."

"Probably not. I'm glad he found someone. We all

deserve happiness." Taylor shivered. Suddenly all her senses were on high alert, the warm fuzzy feeling gone—her head perfectly clear. Owen. For a year she'd constantly looked over her shoulder, worried he might be there. Even after things had settled, he was always in the back of her mind, but never in a good way. Tonight he'd been less than thirty feet away.

Joe noticed her shiver. "Cold?"

"A little. The temperature dropped." Better than admitting that Owen had terrified her at the end of their relationship, so much that she'd called the police. Twice.

"We should probably get back," he suggested. Their pretzel plate boasted crumbs and his beer glass held one last sip, so he lifted the rim to his lips, finished off the brew. "Unless you want anything else? I'm happy to stay longer."

"Cup of black coffee might be good, if you have the time."

"I've got all night."

She relaxed. "Good, because I could use a jolt of caffeine. I'll have no break when I get back."

Leo magically appeared to take the order and remove the dirty dishes.

"Make it two cups black," Joe told him, leaning forward to pass over the empty beer glass. ' So, when can you show me how to take portraits? What's your schedule look like?"

"I don't have my planner with me, but I do have my phone." Taylor scrolled through its calendar. Sadly, most days were empty. Once she met with Virginia on Tuesday, she had very few photo dates. She also had a meeting with the professor supervising her project, the one who'd rejected her time and again.

Maybe Joe was right about karma. Maybe she still owed on some great cosmic bill she didn't know about. Maybe her professor would think that boxing would be project worthy. She could go to the gym . . .

Like her earlier buzz, she let the idea fade away as she sipped the coffee Leo brought. Her professor wanted something that would provide a window into the soul. He'd rejected idea after idea, everything from working with the elderly to a day in the no-kill shelter. Boxing would be too mundane. Not enough of a look into another world. He wanted something beyond the photo story. He wanted something where people allowed themselves to be vulnerable. Where they faced their fears head-on. Something where people exposed themselves without even knowing it, where they let others peer into the depths of their psyche. . . . Like exposing when they'd been burned.

She finally understood what her professor meant. Joe was passionate about making his sister and other burn survivors feel beautiful.

To do that, they'd have to show their skin, their flaws, and own them in a defiant celebration of their bodies. Show that they'd overcome. That fate hadn't won.

She knew for certain that this was something her professor would get behind. She'd have to clear it with him, but it was the best idea she'd had. Come on, karma, she thought. You owe me one.

She glanced up, caught Joe's gaze. "You know what?"

"What?" he asked, taking her bait.

"I'll do it. Your book."

He sat back with a thump. "You will?"

"Yes." As soon as she said the words, she knew she was one hundred percent committed. Even if her project wasn't approved, and she was pretty sure it would be, Joe had gotten under her skin in a way she didn't yet understand. Doing his book meant she'd see him again, and not just one more time like if she photographed his family. She wanted to keep seeing him—she hadn't felt this relaxed or turned on in ages.

After Owen, she'd sworn never again, but Joe made her want to trust, made her want to believe. She could use the publicity the book would provide, she rationalized. Maybe if she moved fast, she'd still have a shot at entering the competition. "I want those networking connections," she told him. "You're right. It'll be a good opportunity."

He reached forward and shook her hand. Her fingertips tingled, sending raw heat coursing through her veins. "Perfect. So we have a new agreement."

"Yes. You. Me. We'll take the photos and produce the book."

"Sounds like a plan."

She laughed at his deliberate choice of words. Each minute she spent in his company made her like him more, made her loosen up, made her want to lose the fearful woman who was once bitten, twice shy. If nothing else, she wanted to feel something that didn't come from a book, indulge in a fantasy even if it was a fool's errand.

She took his hand, gave it another shake. Heat fused

them together, warming her through. She blushed, smiled. Shook her head in disbelief as his lips inched upward in a grin. "You know, Joe, for once you just might be right."

"Really?"

"Yes." His hand felt good. She didn't want to let it go. "I do believe we have a plan."

***

Bill paid—his treat, he'd insisted—Joe found himself a few minutes later once again clinging to the door handle as she sped her little car through the streets of St. Louis. He didn't mind. She'd agreed. A huge load had been lifted from his shoulders.

Sure, he would now have to introduce her to his family, who would immediately love her. That was a small price to pay, for every woman Joe brought around was potential marriage material until proven otherwise. Not that there were many women. Actually more like few and far between.

As for Taylor, she was the photographer. Joe admitted he liked her. She was blunt. Funny. Devoted. Interesting. Sexy as hell, whether her hair was up or down, like now. He glanced at her profile as she whipped around a corner. They were almost back at Presley's. Yes, interesting, and he'd be interested in asking her out, but he refused to complicate matters. Also, all his standard reasons of why he didn't date rushed forward, but Joe pushed them aside. No reason to rehash those. He'd lived a long time with the truth about himself, that his flaws drove women away.

He needed Taylor for the book, and he wanted the book for his sister. So any desires he had needed to be kept in check. No matter how tempting Taylor might be.

She threw the car in park, jolting him, and then they were standing outside her car. "I'll call you." he told her, "for sure this time."

She smiled, the glow of the streetlights lighting up her whole face. "I won't hold my breath."

He had the urge to kiss her, to capture that breath, to draw it from her lips and into his body. Instead, he shoved his hands into his front pockets. "My mother and sister won't let me live it down if I don't. I guess you need to go in. Do you want me to walk you to the door?"

"It's right there. It's safe. I'll be fine."

"Okay." He removed his hands, dropped them to his side. They weren't on a date, and her upturned, expectant face demanded he take charge. He reached forward, tucked a loose stand of hair behind her ear. Her breath hitched. "Good night then."

He thrust his right hand forward, the handshake failing to satisfy the overpowering need to touch her, to explore her softness. Just rubbing his thumb over her lower lip—what would that hurt?

Instead, he fused his fingers with hers, shook, and detached quickly before he did something that would embarrass himself or ruin being professional. Instead, he waited until she had safely entered the restaurant before he turned, took a deep breath, and went home.

Chapter Four

"You know I can't do it without your help. If you don't help me, the entire country could be in jeopardy."

"You know I'll help you, Duncan. How could I not? I—"

"Don't say you love me. I'm a rogue. A rake."

"A spy in the guise of a pirate."

He reached to gently touch her face. "My priority must be saving the crown."

"Good book?"

"Hey Mom." Taylor dog-eared a corner. Sunday afternoon found Taylor making her weekly visit to her mother's house. Unlike Taylor's kitchen cupboards, which contained around two packets of ramen, three microwavable mashed-potato cups, and a half empty box of Pop-Tarts, her mom's pantry was always full. She also stocked vanilla wafers and Oreos. Within seconds of putting down her book, Taylor had a handful of each.

Good cookies always made the weekly Sunday afternoon visit more bearable. Earlier she'd also made herself a roast beef and provolone sandwich, which was basically breakfast and lunch combined.

"You know, if you can't afford food, you can always move home," her mom suggested. She leaned a jean-clad hip against the center island, her short-sleeve kaftan rustling. "Live here and get three squares a day."

"I'm good," Taylor mumbled through an overstuffed mouthful of chocolate and cream filling. She sighed as the delicious goodness rolled over her taste buds. Store brands certainly couldn't compete with the real thing. She set her uneaten cookies on the countertop and reached into an overhead cabinet for a glass.

Anticipating, her mother opened the refrigerator door and passed over a fresh half gallon of milk.

"Thanks." Taylor poured herself a large glass and drank most down in one gulp. Then she refilled.

Her mom's brow creased with worry. "If you're hungry, I can lend you money for groceries, you know. I don't like that you're not eating."

"I eat. Last night I went to Dressel's. I just don't buy cookies. Bad for my figure. Good because it gives me a reason to come see you." Hunger slightly abated, Taylor dunked an Oreo before taking a bite. She wiped her sticky fingers on her jean shorts. "I'm turning in the calendar shoot Tuesday and I'll get paid then. It'll tide me over for a while."

"I just wish you'd let me help. Move back home and save some money. Just for a little while. Maybe being here would help you focus on your project. How's that going?"

"Fine."

Her mom didn't buy her fib. "Honey, I thought you'd have it done by now. I hate that you're spending all this money on a master's. Webster isn't cheap."

"I've got it handled, Mom," Taylor replied stubbornly, as the chocolaty cream temptation on her tongue seemed to say, "Move home and you can eat me every day." She ignored the inner voice and ate a vanilla wafer. "Things are about to break wide open. I've got a new client."

"You need tons of new clients. Charlene knows a person who's got a friend who works at *St. Louis Magazine.* I can find out if they're hiring."

"They aren't. I checked or I'd be all over it. And I've got this."

"I was only trying to help you network." Her mom crossed her arms. Gave her the concerned look Taylor had been seeing for as long as she could remember. "Baby, I don't like seeing you struggle."

"I'm okay, Mom. What's that about it being ninety nine percent persistence?"

Her mom shook her head, disbelieving. "It's 'perspiration.'"

"Same idea."

"You've always been so stubborn."

Taylor's chin jutted forward. "Well, I get it from you. You know you should sell the house and get a condo. Move where there are more people."

Her mom shook her head again. "We've been through this. The house is not too big. And it's paid for. It's centrally located. I can get everywhere in ten minutes."

The one-story, three-bedroom Kirkwood ranch had been the only home Taylor had ever known. The kitchen doorframe had permanent inked lines that marked how tall she and her sister had been on each birthday. Perhaps the memories made her mother lonely, which is why she kept pestering Taylor to move home.

"Yes, but now that Evelyn and I have moved out, it's too much upkeep." Taylor pressed. "You could travel and—"

"The house is not the issue. You'll be taking me out of here in a cardboard box."

"Okay, okay," Taylor replied, backing down. She knew that entrenched tone. "Keep the house. It was Evelyn's idea anyway."

Her mom patted Taylor's arm. "I know you worry, as I do about you. But I'm fine." She reached to wipe some cookie crumbs from the corner of Taylor's lips. "I've got bridge tonight. Oh, I need you to take care of Yin and Yang for me next week."

As if on cue, two fluffy white Himalayans trotted into the kitchen and made figure eights between Taylor's legs, tickling her with their fuzzy tails. "You can stay here while I'm gone. Take care of my babies. It'll only be two days. I'm helping Charlene move her daughter to Topeka. We're taking the car and she's driving the U-Haul."

"Who? Charlene?"

Charlene was even scarier than her mother when it came to driving. Taylor couldn't imagine her behind the wheel of a U-Haul.

Her mother shook her head, her short white hair barely budging. "No. Her daughter. I'm riding shotgun in Charlene's car. We leave Friday. Sheila's accepted an associate job at a legal firm there. Very promising. She can make partner."

Taylor didn't touch that comment, lest she somehow in advertently direct the conversation back toward her own current shortcomings. "I can be here."

"So you'll stay over? I don't want them to be alone. I know it's the weekend, but . . ."

Taylor sighed. She'd walked right into this one. "As long as this isn't a ploy to get me to move home, I'm happy to house sit Yin and Yang."

Her mother feigned innocence. "Never. Although, you may like being home. I'll leave you some homemade meals in the refrigerator."

Taylor resisted rolling her eyes. "Text me the details. I can get to work just as easily from here as I can from my apartment."

"Which is why you should stay here for a while. Save up some money. If the commute's the same—"

"Mom." Taylor rinsed her empty glass and put it in the sink. She washed her hands. "I'd love to discuss this more but I've got photos to process, so I need to get going. I also have another job to plan."

Her mom knew when she'd pushed enough. She opened her arms for a hug and drew Taylor in. "Well, I'm glad you stopped by. I needed a break from being in the garden and I'll need to clean up before bridge."

"One day I should learn that game."

Her mom nodded, leaned back. "You should. I can teach you."

With that, Taylor's mom drew her in for another jasmine-scented hug. As Taylor drove home, her phone rang, and she put it to her ear. "This is Taylor."

"It's Joe."

Joe. His deep sexy voice sent a thrill to her toes, as it had last night. "Hey," she said, her heart racing. Distracted by answering his call, she failed to notice when a car came into her lane. Belated, she honked.

"Are you hands free?"

She frowned, picturing Joe's scowl. "No, but I'm good."

"Do you know how many accidents I work that are caused by driver inattention? Hang up and call me when you're safely parked with the engine off. You've got my number."

With that, he hung up on her. Thoroughly scolded, she tossed the iPhone onto the passenger seat and drummed her fingers on the steering wheel. Really. The man was impossible. Talking on her phone was perfectly legal and she'd never even had so much as a speeding ticket, much less a fender bender.

She pulled into her assigned parking space, the one building amenity she appreciated at four a.m., and walked up three flights of hot stairs. She stepped into her one-bedroom and immediately turned on the window air-conditioning unit. The art deco building in Richmond Heights wasn't centrally cooled, and in the winter the radiators banged and hissed but did a decent job. Still, she loved her space. Her artistic nature had been drawn to large windows that let in copious amounts of natural light. She also loved the high ceilings, the plaster millwork, and the aged wood floors. She flopped onto the couch, letting the cool air blow over her and called Joe back.

"I'm home," she said when he answered, figuring he'd read the caller ID.

"Good. Sorry. Pet peeve. And you're a dangerous driver."

The hair on the back of her neck rose. "I am not."

He laughed, a deep, robust chuckle that did little to reduce her hackles. "You forget I rode with you twice. The first time you had an excuse. The second time not so much."

He let the silence fall, as if picturing her fuming. She refused to dignify him with an answer. "I spoke to my mother," he finally said. "She'd love to have family photos done. We're a go. Also, I want to set up the first of the burn book shoots."

"You move fast."

"In my line of work, you make decisions quickly. No need to waste time. When I see something I want, I go for it, and you are something I want."

She didn't know how to respond to that either. Her skin heated despite being under a direct blast of AC. "Well, okay," she mumbled. "Let me grab my calendar."

She rose, went to the kitchen table, and tugged the Humane Society pocket calendar out of her purse. Having a thing for cats, she'd donated five dollars in response to the direct mailing. The plastic protective cover rustled. "Okay, I just need a pen."

"You don't just use your phone? You scrolled through it last night."

"I do, but only after I write down on hard copy. I always know where my calendar is. I misplace my phone all the time. It's a comedy as I try to find it. Okay, I'm ready." She heard muffled voices in the background, then silence. "Are you there?"

Nothing. No answer.

"Hello? Hello? Are you there?" She checked her phone screen. All five circles were full, so she had more than enough signal. "Hello?"

"Yeah, I'm here." More muffled noise, and then as if the phone was away from his ear, "Yes, I will. Just let me finish this call." She could tell he wasn't talking to her. A few more seconds of silence and he was back. "Sorry about that."

Taylor frowned. "Are you at work?"

"No. Nephew's birthday party. He's four." A pause and then, "Hey! Stop that. I'm on the phone."

She again heard muffled noise. Clearly, Joe didn't have the phone to his ear. "Joe?" She waited. "Joe?"

"What? Yeah. Sorry. My nieces and nephews don't understand that you can't hit a man with a squirt gun when he's on the phone. I should be good now." She heard him exhale a breath. "Maybe not. Can I call you back? I . . . Hey!"

Taylor held her phone out, watched the call timer increase by a second. Then another. Then another. He hadn't ended the call. "Hello?" A female voice came through this time. "Taylor?"

"Yes. This is Taylor."

"Oh, you're there. Good. This is Judy. Judy Marino, Joe's mom. You're the photographer?"

"Yes."

"Wonderful. I absolutely love this idea. I can't wait to meet you." Her enthusiasm came through loud and clear, and Taylor warmed to her immediately.

"Me either. Joe and I were just about to schedule—"

"I'll let you two work out those details, but before we do this, I want to meet you beforehand. In fact, you should probably meet all of us. See what you're getting into. Have you eaten?"

"A small sandwich and some cookies at my mother's." She'd slept until noon, for it'd been hard to sleep after her shift ended. First, she hadn't known how to leave things. After she'd told him she'd do his book, they'd lingered until they'd finished their coffees. Then she'd driven him back to the lot near Presley's, where they'd stood outside her car for a few awkward seconds. Did she hug him? He settled for grabbing her hand and giving it another firm shake.

"A few cookies is not a meal," Judy said. "You need protein. Where are you?"

As if proving Judy's point, Taylor's stomach rumbled.

"I'm at home." She realized belatedly what Judy meant. "Richmond Heights."

"Perfect. We've taken over a huge picnic area just outside the zoo. You know those tables on the hill between the Living World entrance and the Art Museum? We're right there. Look for all the Captain America balloons."

"I . . ." Had Joe's mother just invited her over?

"No need to bring anything," Judy continued. "We have more than enough food. See you in a few. But don't rush. Be safe. Oh, here's Joe."

Within a few seconds, he returned to the line. "Hey. I overheard. So are you coming?"

"Can I say no?"

He chuckled, and she smiled despite herself. "I warned you my mother is a force of nature."

"I'm not sure 'warn' was the word."

"You don't need to come, but it will give you a great opportunity to look us over and decide how the family photo session is going to work. We're all here, and there's a lot of us. It'll also give us a chance to talk."

"I was going to process images from last night and . . ." She glanced at the microwave clock. Almost four. She could spare an hour or two if she burned the midnight oil later. Luckily, she was off Monday.

"So, are you coming? We're grilling pork steaks and there's a very special chocolate birthday cake for dessert."

She shouldn't. She had so much work to do. His rich voice chuckled, as if sensing her inner turmoil. "Don't be chicken. We don't bite."

"Fine," she bit out, strangely not bothered by being coerced into her decision.

"We're literally in the area across from the zoo parking lot. You can't miss us. See you soon."

And with that, the call ended, the timer stopping. Taylor glanced at her red and white striped T-shirt and jean shorts. While the day wasn't boiling, it was hot enough that any makeup would simply melt off. She gave her hair a cursory glance, the St. Louis humidity having frizzed out her curls. She tamed them into a ponytail using a hairband. Then she thrust her calendar back into her purse, shoved her feet into some sandals, and grabbed her camera. She turned her AC down and quickly locked the front door behind her before she second-guessed herself and did exactly what he expected her to do—chicken out.

***

She arrived fifteen minutes later. He hadn't expected her quite so fast, even with his mother telling him that Taylor lived in Richmond Heights, which was practically around the corner. He'd also expected her to call back with some excuse and cancel.

But there was her black Cobalt inching along, and he found himself happily surprised. A small anticipatory jolt shook him, and from his slightly uphill vantage point, he saw her craning her neck as she searched for them. Luckily someone was leaving, so she parked on the street instead of using the zoo lot.

He'd started walking once he'd seen her, so he was waiting a few feet away when she opened the car door. For a moment, the door acted as a shield between them, hiding the part of him that had gone rock hard, because, after Taylor exited she immediately reached back inside, her shorts inching up and her bottom high in the air as she grabbed her camera bag and her purse off the passenger seat. He tightened his fingers on the metal frame in a futile effort to resist the urge to touch. He also mentally recited the Pledge of Allegiance.

She turned to face him, her eyes hidden by wide sunglasses that added seductive mystery. Her hair was up, revealing that long neck he'd first noticed the day of the calendar shoot. He'd found her attractive then, but he'd simply teased her. He'd gotten to know her last night after they'd gone to the hospital. Now, as she swung her camera bag over her shoulder, he realized that maybe he wasn't quite as in control as he thought.

"Can't believe I got this great parking spot," she said in greeting.

"I know. Glad you could make it. We're over here." They walked side by side up the hill to an area of picnic tables. He liked how easily she kept pace. He was starting to like everything about her.

"Your mom wasn't kidding about the balloons. You've got all of the Avengers here."

He hadn't paid much attention. "Ben's only four, so I don't think my brother's let him see any of the movies. But he likes the cartoons."

"There's nothing better than cartoons," Taylor replied, easing into step beside him. She'd seen him walking toward her as she'd driven up, and her breath had hitched. He wore a white polo, jeans, and brown boat shoes, and the combination simply worked. She'd been glad her sunglasses had hidden her widening eyes, and that she'd remembered to close her mouth so she hadn't been gaping. The man was gorgeous, and her heart raced every time he was near.

A tall, dark-haired woman approached, holding out her arms in greeting. "You must be Taylor! I'm Judy, Joe's mom." She drew Taylor in for a hug, then gave her a kiss on both cheeks. "You are just adorable. Come meet the family. Joe, get her something from the cooler. I can't believe you're still standing there. Where are your manners?"

He appeared sheepish. "Soda? Beer?"

After last night, Taylor wanted her wits about her. "A Sprite? 7-Up?"

"We have one of those, I'm sure." Joe went off to find her a beverage while Judy took Taylor's arm and led her over to an area where a group of adults sat.

"I'm so glad Joe thought of doing this," Judy confided as they walked. She pointed. "That's my mother over there, and she's seventy-five. My dad would have been eighty last year, God rest his soul. We should have done these photos yearly while he was alive, but you never think of these things until it's too late, do you? You just think you'll have more time. This is Nana, my husband's mother. Well, Clara, but it's Nana to everyone, including you."

"Hello," Taylor said, as she met Joe's Nana. Then Judy drew her away, and Taylor met so many people, she was grateful she had trained her memory long ago so that she could keep track of them all, at least somewhat.

Joe hadn't exaggerated his family's size: three grandparents still living; two parents; six siblings, three of whom were married; seven nieces and nephews. And that wasn't even counting all the aunts, uncles, and cousins present.

"Is it always like this?" she asked Joe as he brought her a can of Sprite.

"What?"

"So many people?"

"Oh, a lot of them are still at the zoo. They'll be headed over now that it's about to close. You haven't seen anything yet. Overwhelmed?" He gestured to a set of folding lawn chairs and indicated that she should sit. She dropped into the one with the red Cardinals logo on the back.

"Not overwhelmed. More absorbing everything. I've shot weddings before. Compared to some, your family will be a piece of cake."

"Even with all the kids?"

"Well, once a groom and his best man got into a throwdown right before the vows. The father of the bride literally had to pull them apart."

"That sounds like a crazy time."

"Pretty much. To this day I still don't know the reason, and the groom said his 'I do' with a bloody lip. By the reception all was well again and the two were all hugs and smiles."

"Well, we're just a big blue-collar Italian family. We see each other a lot and everyone shows up. There's always some birthday or something, and if I'm not at the station, I'm here."

She liked how family oriented he was. That commitment was one of the things that had swayed her to say yes. "My parents were both only children, as were their parents," Taylor said. "We've always done things on a small scale. Minute actually."

"That's a shame. I hope it means you and your sister are close."

"Close enough," Taylor said. "But she's always busy with her husband's family."

"Uh-oh." Joe glanced over Taylor's shoulder. "Here comes my mom holding a plate. Italians are big on feeding people. Get ready."

Judy handed Taylor a blue plastic plate covered with chips, cheese sauce, and salsa. "Don't want your stomach grumbling. Marvin's about done grilling, so when everyone gets back we'll eat."

"Oh, I'm fine, thanks . . ." Taylor began but Judy had already moved off after shoving the plate into her hand.

Joe grinned and gestured to the food. "She's an expert in the sleight of hand so be warned. She's also a member of the 'you must be starving' club. She'll feed you whether you want it or not."

"I am a little hungry," Taylor admitted, dipping a chip

into the cooling queso. "As I'm on a budget, I'm all about free food."

He laughed and brought the beer can to his mouth. She averted her eyes as if searching. Safer than watching those luscious lips. "Is your sister here? I don't remember meeting Susie."

"She's at the zoo with Winnie and the birthday boy. She'll be over soon and I'll introduce you then. That's why you haven't seen her or most of the kids. You like kids?"

"Doesn't everyone?" She hedged. She knew very little about kids, having never really babysat either. 'I do a lot of childhood environmental portraits, you know the ones taken outside instead of against a fake or plain studio backdrop? Parents want more than just that shot you get at the start of the school year."

He stole a tortilla chip from her plate, scooped up some cheese. "So what do you envision for my family?"

"What were *you* thinking?"

He laughed and covered his mouth quickly as he still had food inside. He swallowed. "A question. I almost forgot your bad habit."

"It's not about *my* vision. It's about yours," she protested. "While I'll help you, you need to decide how many combinations you want, or if you want the pictures inside or outside. I can do formal poses or informal or—" She handed him the plate and reached for the camera bag. "Let me show you."

"The first lesson?"

She smiled. "Perhaps, if you're good."

"I'm always very good." The corner of his lips tilted upward.

"I bet you are," Taylor murmured to herself, safely hidden behind her camera. She pushed her sunglasses up on her head. A light breeze blew. Under the trees, the summer day was actually very nice, the extreme heat rampant earlier in the week having lessened slightly, at least in the shade. She peered through the viewfinder, surveying the scene, then made some adjustments and pressed the shutter. After about ten shots, she held out the camera so Joe could check her work.

"They're nothing fancy," she said, as he scanned through the shots.

"Perhaps not, but you have the right touch," he said. "They're good."

His praise made her face color. She averted her gaze, lest he see. "Now it's your turn. Here, let me show you a few things."

She stood and moved behind him. If she thought she'd be safer there, she was wrong. Being this close meant she inhaled the woodsy scent of wholesome, virile male, making her body jump to attention. She reached over his shoulder, her arm skimming his polo as she laced the camera strap over his neck. He craned his neck, facing her, his lips mere inches from hers. All she had to do was lower her mouth. One, two, three and . . .

She froze, resisted the urge. Her command came out a rasp. "Turn off review mode."

He did.

She'd taught many people how to take photos, but none had made her body wanton. She . . . had . . . to . . . focus. Concentrate on the steps she knew so well. "Look through the viewfinder."

He moved the camera in front of his right eye. She saw Nana in conversation with his mother. She put her hands gently on his head, right above his ears, feeling the silky strands she'd been dreaming about as she guided him to face his first subject. She resisted the urge to weave her fingers deeper, draw his head back, and kiss him from behind.

Thankfully her voice worked, even though it squeaked once. "Now, adjust the lens. One thing you want to do is think of a tic-tac-toe board. Put the center of visual interest in one of the places the lines intersect."

He moved his left hand to the lens, keeping the camera and shutter button balanced with his right. "No, too far." She put her hand on his, moved the lens to where she wanted it, and ignored the shock of awareness that touching him caused. "This setting is better. It should blur out the background, give you a shallow depth of field."

"It does."

She lifted her hand, the heat immediately leaving. However, she rubbed her hands together to dull the sensitivity. He depressed the shutter halfway to focus. "That's great," he said, giving an appreciative whistle as he made the shot.

"You whistling at me, boy?"

"No, Nana," Joe called. "Although you are lovely

today as always."

"Flatterer. Behave yourself over there." Nana shook her head, went back to her conversation. Then Joe lowered the camera so he could see the image on the viewing screen. Taylor still stood behind him, and he swiveled in the lawn chair so he could hold out the camera, strap still around his neck.

"See how it fills the frame and gets rid of the junk in the background?" Taylor asked.

"Yes. I've wanted to know how to do that. Thanks for your help."

"I'm not sure how much you know," she admitted.

"Only what I've figured out by reading online. I'm not very good using the manual mode, and the auto mode focuses on everything all the way back."

"It does, which is why manual's all I shoot. You could also try the aperture priority mode."

"I know the button, but not how to use it. Teach me?" He shot her a hopeful look. His lips parted.

She stammered, "Uh . . . you'll teach yourself. I'll be your coach. It's included in the portrait fee I quoted."

"Deal." He winked and she flushed. She liked his smile far too much.

"Let's try a few more, shall we?" She moved around to the side and reached for his hand, then afraid to touch him again, she gestured instead. He stood, camera strap secure on his neck and device fitted squarely in his hand. He towered over her. "How about you capture your dad grilling?" she suggested, body hyperaware.

"Okay."

They stopped about ten feet from where Joe's dad worked over a large metal grill that stood about waist high. He looked up and grinned at them, and then turned his attention back to basting the pork steaks and turning the hot dogs. Because the charcoal grill rested on a round metal pipe secured in a concrete pad, they could see some of his Bermuda shorts, his bare legs, and flip-flop-covered feet. His "Kiss the Cook" apron was stained with barbeque sauce splotches and hid most of his faded fire department T-shirt and shorts.

"How should you hold the camera?" Taylor asked.

"Vertical shot," Joe said, seeking Taylor's confirmation.

"That's what I'd do. I like how he's in flip-flops. Adds contrast."

Joe turned the camera sideways, gazed through the viewfinder. Adjusted the lens. Then passed the camera to Taylor, their fingers touching for a brief second. "Are those settings right?

She glanced through them and handed back the SLR. Again, his fingers lingered on hers, caressing the tops of her knuckles. "Yes, try that." She swallowed the start of a hiccup, her body's annoying outlet for nerves For he did make her nervous, in that heightened, quivering sort of anticipatory way that indicated high attraction.

"Be sure you get my good side," his dad called. Busy squirting water on a flame after some barbeque sauce dropped onto the hot coals, he didn't even glance up.

"I'll see what I can do," Joe called, squatting low. His

head was even with her waist, meaning his mouth was even with her . . . She stepped backward, checking that erotic thought. The long dry spell post-Owen was coming back to haunt her at the most inopportune time.

He shot several frames, and then made a minor adjustment before taking more. He straightened when finished and passed the camera over. He leaned over her shoulder, his scent again filling her senses, and she found it hard to concentrate. She scrolled through the previews. "There are some keepers in here. You have potential."

He put his hand on his chest. Pouted. "Potential. Gee."

"Such an ego." Taylor laughed. "If you were an expert, you wouldn't need me here."

He looked heavenward. "You wound me, but who can argue with such logic?"

"Certainly not you." She held the camera out. "Want to try again?"

"Pork steaks are done. Food's ready," Marvin called. He waved his spatula. "Get plates and eat it while it's hot."

"Let's postpone for just a bit," Joe said.

"Okay."

He placed a hand on the small of her back and guided her toward the serving tables. She tried not to tremble. It was a polite gesture, nothing more, but his touch still sent quivers through her. She swallowed another hiccup, warning her traitorous body to calm down.

"There's Susie."

A group of women and kids headed up the hill. She

recognized Susie immediately, for she was the one covered up. Despite the steady breeze, she had to be hot. Even though she wore a tank top, she'd topped it with a light plaid fabric, long-sleeve top that she wore over a pair of faded blue jeans.

A girl about three held onto her hand. "That's Susie and Winnie," Joe confirmed. He handed Taylor a paper plate of full food. "In this family, you snooze, you lose," he told her. "The only ones safe around here are the kids. They're getting hot dogs."

She assumed he was joking as there appeared to be more than enough food. "You eating something too?"

He grinned. "Yep." He gestured to a cloth-covered table. "Have a seat. Be right back."

She plopped down on the picnic bench and set her plate down. The action allowed her time to study Joe's family. The full crowd had arrived. Winnie giggled, held aloft on dad Parker's shoulders. Susie laughed at something as she filled a plate and handed it to her husband. Then they joined Taylor at the table. Seconds later, Joe sat down with his own loaded plate.

"So you're the photographer," Parker said.

"Taylor," Joe offered, grabbing a clear plastic knife.

"Taylor," Winnie parroted, a smear of barbeque sauce from her hot dog already on her lips.

"That's me," Taylor replied. She cut some of her pork steak and popped the bite into her mouth. Delicious.

"Joe tells me you've agreed to help him with the book," Parker continued.

Mid swallow, Taylor nodded.

"I like books," Winnie said.

"We know you do," Susie said. "Mouth closed when you chew. We're working on manners." She shot Taylor an apologetic smile.

Winnie closed her mouth with an exaggerated snap, and Taylor stifled a chuckle. Winnie was adorable, around the age Taylor's niece would have been. At least Evelyn had tried again, and Taylor had an adorable eight-month-old niece. "It's fine."

Susie wiped Winnie's mouth, and for the first time Taylor could see clearly the scar tissue on the back of Susie's hands. "So what are your plans for the photos?" Susie asked.

"Joe and I haven't talked in detail yet, but my goal is always to make everyone feel comfortable and beautiful. High fashion but with no rough edges. Either on a backdrop or perhaps in a favorite environment. Joe and I have a lot to discuss."

Susie pushed her brown bangs off to the side. "Okay, I have no idea what any of that means, but I'd like to be comfortable."

"I promise you will be," Taylor said, meaning every word. She lifted her fork to spear some green beans.

"She'll do a good job," Joe affirmed. "We're going to talk this week and work out the details. I told you about last night, and how sensitive Taylor was."

"You did," Susie affirmed. "Joe says you're a good person. He told me about your hospital work."

He had? Taylor had no idea how to respond, but luckily, Winnie pulled on her mom's sleeve. "Mommy. I have to go potty."

"Duty calls," Susie said, beginning to extricate herself from the picnic table.

Taylor stood, stepped over the bench. "I'll come with you."

Joe arched an eyebrow. She'd hardly touched anything on her plate. "You know that thing about women not able to go alone," Taylor joked. She joined Susie, who was already hustling Winnie to a nearby restroom.

Taylor availed herself of the facilities, washed her hands, and waited by the sink as Winnie and Susie finished up in larger, handicapped stall.

"I didn't have an accident," Winnie proudly told Taylor as her mom held her up so she could wash her hands.

"That's a big girl," Taylor replied.

Winnie grinned widely and waved her hands under the hot-air dryer. "All done, Mommy."

On the way back, once they got close enough to the picnic area, Susie allowed Winnie to run on ahead. Taylor used the opportunity to ask the question that had been bothering her. "Are you okay with this?"

"What do you mean?" Susie asked.

"The book. The photos. Your brother can be a bit . . ." Taylor hesitated, trying to find the politically correct word.

"Bullheaded?" Susie filled in with a laugh. Eyes similar to Joe's twinkled.

"I don't know if I'd go that far. But Joe is pretty determined."

"Oh, you've just met him. You've seen nothing yet. He's as stubborn as they come."

"He did tell me he likes challenges," Taylor admitted.

"That's an understatement. You're talking about a guy who can complete the crosswords in the *New York Times* in record time. He's killer at Sudoku. But back to your original question. I actually think the book is a good idea. People who've been burned carry a very visible reminder of a terrible accident. We look in the mirror and see scars. Most people complain about their looks, but many of us struggle to ever see any beauty at all. If your photos can give us a glimpse of that, I'm all for doing this. For once, I want to be out of the shadows and not feel disfigured or think I need to hide my skin so it doesn't disgust people."

Taylor felt her eyes moisten. She blinked. "Thanks for being so honest with me. If I had any residual doubts about this project, you've ended them. I've got some ideas brewing that I'll discuss with Joe."

"Have you asked him about why this is so passionate to him? Why he's so determined?"

The question caught Taylor off guard. "No."

"You really should ask him."

"He told me a bit about what happened when you were little. That he couldn't save you."

Susie's brow rose. "Wow. I'm surprised. That's more than what he normally shares."

Taylor paused. "There's more?"

"He'll tell you when he's ready," Susie said, giving Taylor absolutely no clue to what she meant.

They were almost back to the picnic area. Winnie was sitting on Parker's lap and Joe was making silly faces at her. He reached forward and tweaked her nose, and then showed her his thumb tucked between his forefingers as if he'd stolen it. Winnie reached up and touched her nose to make sure it was there, and then laughed.

"He's such a great uncle," Susie said, oblivious to the sudden tumult overtaking Taylor as Winnie reached up and "stole" Joe's nose.

Getting personally involved with her clients was not allowed. She needed to close her heart. Listen to her head. Shut out these silly emotions that threatened to disturb her existence. Yet as she rejoined the group at the picnic table and lifted her fork, she realized that any defense system she deployed would be far too little, and far too late.

Chapter Five

Taylor looked like she was having fun. As Joe spooned a corner piece of birthday cake through his lips, he allowed his nervousness to fade. She hadn't run for the hills. He dipped the spoon into the vanilla ice cream and took another bite.

Across the way, his thirty-two-year-old sister Liz wanted to know if Taylor could do a separate family portrait of her, her husband, and their three kids at a later time. She and Taylor were discussing the logistics.

"I like her," Susie said.

"I'm not planning on dating her," Joe replied.

Susie gave him a knowing smile that said *Gotcha*. "Did I say anything about dating? You made that leap and stuck your foot in that admission all by yourself. Thanks for confirming you've thought about her beyond photography. Hmm. I wonder what Mom would think?"

"Damn," Joe said, setting his empty Captain America cake plate down. "You'll keep quiet."

"Maybe," Susie teased.

"She's attractive," Joe admitted. "I'd be blind not to see that."

"You'd be a fool not to do anything, especially if you like her," Susie countered.

"I like her, but we're working together. The last thing I want is to have the book derailed by romantic complications."

"Sometimes those are the best kind."

"Not for me." He eyed her. "Did you say anything to Taylor?"

Susie shook her head. "No. It's not my story to tell."

Joe ran a hand through his hair. She'd kept his secret. "Thanks."

"You have to forgive yourself sometime, you know," she told him. "I've forgiven you."

"Well it's hard to forget when you're faced with the daily reminder," he shot back.

"You can choose to look at it or look past it. When I finally let go, along came Parker. He sees me, not my scars. And we have Winnie. And"—she paused, leaned closer—"another one's on the way."

A thrill shot through him. "Really? You're . . . ?"

"Almost ten weeks. We've just been waiting for the right moment."

"What about now?"

"It's Ben's birthday."

"He's four. He's not going to care."

"I don't want to steal Claire's thunder."

Steve, their brother and Claire's husband, approached the table. "What are you two talking about?"

"Susie and Parker have an announcement but they don't want to steal Ben's thunder."

Eyes so like Susie's and Joe's widened in comprehension. "That's great! Claire won't mind. Hey Parker!" he called. "Get over here."

Seeing her husband, Claire also came over.

Taylor followed. She came to stand by Joe, and he liked having her there. Even after just a few hours, she seemed like she belonged. "What's going on?" she asked.

Parker ambled over. "Yeah?"

"You need to tell everyone the news," Steve said.

"What news?" Claire asked. The light dawned quickly. "Oh my god! Susie! Congrats! This is so exciting!"

Taylor turned to Joe. "Am I missing something?"

He realized she couldn't yet follow the way his family could communicate without words. "Susie's pregnant."

"Oh. Congrats!" Taylor said.

Soon the entire family was congratulating Susie and Parker, allowing Joe and Taylor to ease back from the crowd. "Exciting," she said.

"I'm always ready to be an uncle," Joe said.

'I know. It's fun. My sister did try again, and Allie is almost one."

"That's good." He shoved his hands into his jeans pockets. "Thanks for coming today. It meant a lot to my mom." And me, he thought but didn't voice.

"You're welcome. It was a good idea. Not only did you

bring me more business, as promised, but I have tons of ideas for your family portrait and, after talking with Susie, no reservations about doing your book."

He grinned. Music to his ears. "Great. Shall we make plans? Could we book Friday for the first shoot?"

"Let me look." Joe watched as Taylor retrieved her purse and withdrew her calendar. "I can do Friday."

"Great. Pencil me in. I'll line up the first person."

"Okay." She yawned. "Sorry. Long night again, and I have to burn the midnight oil on the photos. My deadline's Tuesday."

Concern filled him. She had work to do. "Why don't you go home, and we'll talk later this week? I'm working Tuesday and Wednesday but off after that."

"That will work. I'm glad you called me. And the food and cake weren't too bad either." She smiled, and it was like a punch in the gut. He wanted her. Badly.

"I'll walk you to your car when you're ready," Joe said, trying to maintain a safe distance.

"I am getting a little sensory overloaded, and I have a lot of work to do." Taylor agreed. A group of shrieking kids ran past, and almost knocked her over.

Joe reached out to steady her, drawing her close to his chest where she seemed to fit perfectly. He searched her face, those perfect pink lips far too close to his. "You okay?"

"Yeah. Just knocked off balance."

Someone whistled. "Get a room you two."

"You're funny, Steve," Joe yelled to his brother. "How about you control your kids before they knock people over?"

"Joe. Be nice to your brother." And before Steve could open his mouth to add something, their mother added, "And Steve, Taylor is our guest. She shouldn't just be knocked down."

"Kids, go play over there," Joe's dad shouted, and every grandchild immediately complied. He then went back to cleaning the grill.

"I'm fine," Taylor said, smoothing her shorts and smiling at everyone. "No worries here."

However, Joe wasn't fine. Having her pressed against him had disturbed his equilibrium. He'd felt heated—and from far more than the afternoon sun. He'd started to sweat—not the kind that dripped, but the type where wanton skin slicked into silk. A part of him tried to stretch the front of his jeans. He wasn't a teenage boy, but in that moment he'd felt like one, like the first time he'd held a girl in his arms.

He needed to get a grip.

Taylor made the rounds to say her good-byes, receiving hugs and kisses on both cheeks from his parents and from Nana. She accepted each with grace.

"She's better than that last woman you dated," Susie whispered. "The one who only air kissed."

"That was . . ." Joe couldn't remember. Had it been that long since he'd dated anyone seriously? He'd simply been so busy and, without anyone to capture his interest, there'd been no real point. Steve had done his job to ensure the Marino name would continue, so that responsibility was off Joe's back.

"Joe, ready?" Taylor called.

"Yep."

She slung her camera bag and purse over her shoulder, and then they began to walk down the hill to her car, aware that most of his family watched their entire progress.

"We have an audience," Joe said.

She swiveled, glanced over her shoulder, and gave a final, friendly wave. "Your family is sweet."

"You saw us on a good day."

"No, seriously. We are nowhere near as tight, and it's a shame. I'm going to need to work on that. What time will everyone leave?"

Joe glanced at his wristwatch. A little after six thirty. "Probably in another hour. The kids will need baths and then it'll be bedtime."

"True. We always had an early bedtime, which is ironic as now I stay up into the wee hours working."

"Try to get some sleep tonight."

"I have to get the images done for Virginia. If I fail, I don't get paid and my mother will insist I live with her. As it is, she has me housesitting her Himalayans for two nights next week so she can help a friend and her friend's daughter on some cross-county moving adventure. She's hoping that by having me stay in my childhood bedroom, I'll be enticed to move back home."

They reached her car, and Taylor put her camera in her trunk. She walked around and opened the driver's door, and pent-up hot air whooshed out. She started the engine, cranked the AC, and then climbed back out, shutting the door and leaning her hip on it. "We'll let that cool down."

"Smart idea."

She hadn't put on her sunglasses, so facing west, she held up a hand to shade her eyes. She saw a flicker there. "Oh no. You've had those calls. They weren't—"

"One was," he confirmed, surprised he was sharing with her. "Two-year-old in his car seat."

"Oh, Joe." Her hand came down and touched his arm. He could see tears threaten her eyes. He shifted, blocking the sun. "I'm so sorry." She blinked, trying to hold back the flow.

He crooked a finger, tucked it under her chin. "It's my job."

"I couldn't do it." She bit her lip, put both hands on his forearms.

"But you did last night," he reminded her. Her touch comforted him, broke through the shell he'd erected around himself. She was dangerous.

"But I know they can't be saved."

"So do we, before we even get the door open."

She shivered as the tears escaped. "How does it not give you a form of PTSD?"

Any other woman who'd asked him this had met with anger. He was a protector. He didn't need help. Didn't need sympathy. Yet, with Taylor, he wanted to talk. Wanted to let her in, no matter how scary the prospect. "Maybe it does," he admitted. "I've found physical activity is the best release. I'm rock climbing tomorrow." He moved his fingers—wiped her tears away.

"I'd be afraid I'd fall off," she said, stopping the sniffles.

"There are ropes. I'll take you."

She shook her head. "Nope. Afraid of heights. Made one attempt at rappelling during Girl Scouts and I was done."

"So no jumping out of airplanes either." He'd diverted her attention, and she laughed.

"Heck no."

"You should probably go before you use all your gas," Joe said. "It's cool in there."

"Or good enough," she replied. She lifted her hands, missing the skin-to-skin contact. "Thank you for today. Thank you for the jobs. I feel like I have some egg on my face for being so stubborn about things at first."

"It's part of your charm," he told her, reaching around her to open the car door. If she didn't get inside soon, he was going to do something foolish, like kiss her senseless, which would be doubly foolish with his entire family watching. "We'll talk this week."

"I look forward to it." She slid into the car. "Tell your family I enjoyed meeting them."

"I will." He shut her door, stood rooted until she'd backed up and driven away. As he turned to head up the hill, Parker came down with a cooler and put it in a silver minivan two spaces down.

"Are we calling it a day?" Joe asked.

"Starting to," Parker said. "We have to be at the early church service, so it's almost past our bedtime."

"I better go help clean up then," Joe said.

Forty minutes later, he parked his pickup in the tiny parking lot of his St. Louis Hills apartment and climbed the stairs to the second floor. He dropped his keys and iPhone on the corner of the TV stand. Immediately his fat orange tiger-striped cat came to rub against his jeans. Brutus's automatic feeder had gotten low, and Joe refilled the dry kibble and refreshed the automatic waterer. Brutus immediately stuck his head under the flow. When Joe worked, his sister Elaina, who lived across the hall with her roommate Megan, took care of the cat Joe had found as a kitten outside a burned-out building.

Sometimes Joe wasn't sure who owned the apartment, him or Brutus. He rubbed his hand across the back of his neck, the stickiness of the day evident. He started the shower—the old building's hot-water heater needing an extra minute to heat up—and stripped down, easing his jeans inside out.

As he did, his fingers eased over why he refused to wear anything but long pants, the real reason he'd joined the family profession, and the major impediment to his love life. He might be Mr. September from the waist up, but from mid-thigh down he sported puckered, wrinkled skin that would never feel smooth, never be anything but tight and discolored. His first girlfriend had blanched and brought her hand to her mouth when she'd seen him naked. Needless to say, he'd been a late bloomer in the sex department, and he'd never once turned on the light.

He stepped under the spray, letting the hot water wash away the day's grime. Tomorrow he had a full day of rock climbing and at least two hours' worth of boxing practice. The male-dominated ring was the only place he felt comfortable in shorts, but yet, when he competed, he wore a custom-made pair with a hem just below the knees. When he added in his lucky socks, his legs were pretty much covered.

He ran shampoo through his hair, working the suds through the thick strands. He let his mind drift, picturing Taylor's pretty face. He'd been so close to kissing her. He'd seen the interest flickering in her hazel eyes. All he would have had to do was lean forward and bring his mouth down on that perfect pink bow. She'd even parted her lips slightly. . . . Part of him quickened and he shook his head under the spray, sending a line of suds racing down his torso as he rinsed. As he ran soap over his scarred legs, the thought of kissing Taylor quickly fizzled.

He sensed she might be different, but deep down he knew that when she saw him, she'd be like all the others. First she'd be shocked. Repulsed. Then she'd turn sympathetic. Nurturing. Then overbearing and controlling, as if that could somehow save him.

It was twenty years too late for that.

He turned off the water, stepped from the shower, and wiped the steam from the mirror. He gazed at himself in the condensation-covered glass, his features distorted.

He needed to remain professional around Taylor. She was ten years younger than him. She didn't need an older, damaged man. He had to remain professional. They had a book to complete, and despite any other interest in her, that had to be enough.

After a lifetime of rejection, he couldn't risk anything else.

Chapter Six

Taylor hadn't expected Virginia to bring her entourage to Tuesday's photo viewing, but given the gaggle of woman present at the model shoot, she really shouldn't have been surprised. However, today the number of onlookers had doubled, and Taylor's fingers trembled as she hooked her laptop to the LCD projector. Unlike when she'd met one-on-one in Virginia's office to sign the contract, she stood in big conference room of Perlow, Barker and Wayman, Virginia's husband and son's legal firm and home base for Virginia's charity work. Taylor ran a hand over her best skirt, a black and white cotton checkerboard A-line Armani skirt that she'd paired with a black fitted top. She'd found both at the resale shop with tags still on for a fraction of the original price.

This must be the full charity committee, Taylor thought, as the LCD projected her laptop's desktop onto the screen. She clicked the file and took a deep breath. "I've put these in monthly order, and given you a range of shots to choose from for each one."

"Good, I'm glad of that." Virginia leaned back in a leather conference chair that probably cost more than a month of Taylor's rent. Virginia sat at the head of the table, closest to the screen and pressed a remote. The lights dimmed. "Let's see what you've got."

Taylor began. "This is Mr. January, Blaine Johnson. You'll see I've put him in Carondelet Park at the Boathouse. I chose this instead of Forest Park so we could showcase the city's third-largest park."

"The lighting is fabulous," said a woman near the end of the table.

"Look how good he looks," said another.

"Too bad I'm married," added a third.

"I like it," Virginia declared, and with a wave, she urged Taylor on. "Good choice. Let's see the rest of Mr. January's shots."

Taylor inhaled, and moved to the next picture. As she progressed month by month, she slowly began to relax. The women seemed pleased, each making comments and notations on a sheet as to which photos they liked from each month's set.

"Ah, here he is," Virginia said as Taylor displayed the first of Joe's photos. "He was our last one."

"I remember him," a woman down the table called. "Women will want to burn their houses down to meet this one."

Blown up on the screen, Joe appeared larger than life. Taylor had fought with the backgrounds, finally settling for one of the plainer choices, an industrialized setting that was deliberately out of focus so that Joe dominated the frame. She swallowed. He was ratings gold.

"He wears that gear well," a woman commented, reaching for her water glass. "He's going to be a magnet for the calendar ball."

"Oh yes, you are planning on attending that, right Taylor?" Virginia asked. "I'll have my assistant get you the information now that we've set an early November date and locked in the Chase Park Plaza hotel as a venue. We'll be launching the calendar that night, and all the men will be present. You should be there as well. Black tie."

"I'd be happy to attend." She'd have to start saving for an appropriate dress, but the event was months away. Plenty of time. She flipped to the next slide.

"It's hard to decide on this one," a voice called. "Can I see the first one again?"

"I liked the third," someone called.

"I like them all," added someone else. "He'll definitely be a hit."

A clamor began. "I'm glad you mussed his hair. Gives him an after-bed look."

"If I wasn't married, I'd take him to bed."

"Didn't you say that about that last few guys?"

"A girl can dream."

"Ladies," Virginia said, ending the chatter that was fast making Taylor uncomfortable. It had been hard enough editing Joe's pictures. Often she'd zoomed in so he was simply a bunch of pixels, too close to see the full picture as she worked. The man took a great photograph. He was even better in person, and she could remember how his hair felt as if she'd just touched it, instead of two days ago.

"They're all great," Virginia said in a way that Taylor knew there was a "but" coming. "But these are missing something. There was a spark, a sexiness to the shoot. Let me see the raw images from the end."

"I . . ."

"Show me," Virginia commanded, and Taylor sighed and clicked on a different file folder.

"Let me show you this one." Taylor dragged a photo into Photoshop and brought it up full-screen. An image of Joe flashed up on the screen, and immediately the women gasped.

"Yes. That's the one I want," Virginia said. "You should have shown me that one first."

Taylor didn't even attempt an excuse. While she'd digitally enhanced this photo, she hadn't included it among the five she'd presented for the simple reason that it was her best shot, and upon seeing it finished, she'd immediately wanted to keep it private.

"He could grace the cover of *GQ*," a woman tittered.

"Or Playgirl."

Which was exactly why she'd held it back. His head was slightly tilted, and he had both hands on the edges of his jacket, as if about to rip it off. Those blue-gray-green eyes smoldered, and his lips inched in promise. The overall impression was that he was about to strip and join a woman in bed, and that when he did, it was going to be very, very good.

The photo was intimate, sexy. The part of him she longed to see, especially after being close enough to kiss him. Crazy women would come out of the woodwork after having him displayed on their wall for thirty days. He was a fixer—the type of guy who would come to your aide and solve all problems—and this photo would thrust him into the spotlight in ways he probably hadn't anticipated when he'd been coerced into being Mr. September.

"I knew you were the right person for the job," Virginia said, giving Taylor a smile. "Now that month nine is settled, let's see the rest."

Taylor ignored the little fission of guilt. Even though he'd indicated he'd had no choice, Joe had agreed to the shoot and she needed the job. She began to show the other photos. Virginia and crew loved the rest, and soon the lights were back on and Taylor uploaded the chosen photos to a flash drive.

"Wonderful work," Virginia said, passing over the check. Taylor placed the envelope in her purse. "You can be sure I will be recommending you."

"I appreciate that."

"What are you working on next?"

"Actually, I'm taking Joe Marino's family portraits."

Virginia pushed her reading glasses onto her head. "I *thought* he had a thing for you during the photo shoot."

Taylor tried not to blush. "No, it's nothing like that. He wanted help with a charity book for the Burns Recovered Support Group. He needed a photographer.

Someone who would work pro bono. The family photo job is to make up for the pro bono stuff."

"Well, he's quite the hottie. Is that the current word?" Virginia laughed and shrugged. "You should pursue that."

"We're professionals." Although Taylor's face reddened.

"Did I ever tell you how my husband and I met? I worked in his office. I was a young paralegal. Basically in the typing pool. But I saw him and knew he was to be mine. Now I've got grandchildren and a great-grandchild on the way and we just celebrated fifty years. So you go for it."

Taylor couldn't help but smile. "I'll remember that."

"You do that," Virginia said, patting her on the arm. "Now, my son is taking me to a late lunch. It's so kind of him to let me run my charity work from here."

"I'm sure he likes having you close," Taylor said as a forty-something man stepped into the room.

"Ready Mom?"

"Just about," Virginia replied, placing the flash drive in her purse. The entourage had somehow faded away, off to whatever woodwork they'd emerged from. "Thank you again, Taylor. I'm intrigued your new project. Let me know if I can help. I'm always looking for another charity to support. And if you do win your man, you call me. I know the perfect wedding planner."

Butterflies jumped in Taylor's stomach as she held back a hiccup. "That's very premature."

"You never know." Virginia shook Taylor's hand, then

followed her son from the conference room.

Taylor reached into her purse and turned her phone ringer on. She'd missed two calls and had one text, from a number she didn't recognize. She swiped, read the text, and frowned. "I really need to see you. Please."

He'd signed it.

Owen.

Her fingers shook as she deleted the text. Why was he bothering her? He'd clearly been on a date the other night. Joe had thought it appeared serious. Whatever Owen had to say, it didn't matter.

She didn't want to hear it. Would never want to hear it. She wanted nothing to do with him.

So how had he gotten her number anyway? After their breakup, she'd changed phone numbers—a long process where she'd probably lost several potential clients who'd been unable to reach her. Staying far from Owen was the reason she didn't even have a web site or do social media.

Fingers still trembling, she listened to her voice mails as she walked to her car. Both were from her mother, reminding her about house sitting on Friday. She'd call her mom back once the check was in the bank. Heck, being in a good mood from knowing her rent and bills would be paid for the next month or so, maybe she'd even stop by.

***

"So, she agreed to do your burn book?"

"Isn't that something like high school students do?"

Reid asked, saving Joe from replying. "Like in *Mean Girls*?"

As part of a training drill, Kyle angled the Jaws of Life and cut through the A-frame on the driver's side of a crumpled Chevy sedan. Kyle shouted over the din. "Reid, you saw *Mean Girls*?"

"Yeah, I did, so what of it?" Reid's gloved hands pulled the cut metal out of the way. "Remember my sister is eight years younger. It was on cable. I was doing my brotherly duty in hanging out with my sis. Doesn't hurt that Rachel McAdams is hot."

"He'll never admit it, but he watched it all by himself," Chris threw out, his own Jaws of Life cutting through the A-frame on the passenger side. Joe waited for Reid, and then together the two of them peeled the roof of the car upward. "Almost there," Joe called, a bead of sweat trickling down the back of his neck.

As part of their routine drills, he and his team wore full turnout gear, this morning practicing vehicle extrications on crumpled cars in the back lot of Kent's Salvage and Parts. They'd been cutting through metal for most of the morning, each taking turns with the various tools they'd use in a real accident. Thankfully the morning had been quiet. Had a call come in, they would have immediately been in the truck, rolling out.

The roof removed, Joe signaled for a break. "Good work. And yeah, she's agreed to help. Told you Marino charm wouldn't fail."

Kyle powered off the Jaws of Life, the sudden lack of noise allowing the pleasant sounds of the summer day to reach their ears. Now on their fifth extrication—or was it their sixth?—they'd begun to loosen up, losing the earlier extreme seriousness and intensity of the first two. As a unit, they'd been together for a while, and required drills kept them fresh, like Joe's boxing practices kept him ready for the ring and his daily runs kept him prepped for the marathons.

After they finished this last extrication, they could head back to the firehouse. "She must be desperate if she's falling for that Marino charm."

"Nah, she just knows a good thing when she sees it," Joe joked.

"And he's not even paying her," Chris added.

"Well, he could give her these." Reid reached into the car and onto the floor in front of the passenger seat. He held up a pair of hot pink panties. "Looks like we hit pay dirt today." The thin fabric of the thong dangled from Reid's gloved forefinger.

"Put those down," Joe ordered, but he couldn't help but laugh with the guys. You never know what you'll find when you cut into junkyard cars.

Chris laughed. "Lieutenant, you could wash these up and—"

"You're not going to like what I'm going to do to you if you continue speaking," Joe threatened, and Chris wisely shut his mouth. Still, laughter edged the lips of all his men, and finally Joe threw his gloved hands up. "Fine. That's damn funny."

They all then roared with laughter.

"So are you serious about her?" Reid asked, tossing Joe the panties, which he caught perfectly.

"It's not a date. She's just helping out on the book." He tossed them back into the car.

"So much for the Marino charm," Kyle said.

"You don't go out on enough dates," Chris threw out. He'd become engaged over the weekend. So far none of them had let him live it down.

"I'm not ready for the old ball and chain like you," Joe replied.

"Hey, I wasn't getting any younger. You aren't either, lieutenant," Chris responded.

"I could ask her out. I saw her at the restaurant. She was your waitress," Reid said. "She's like, what, *my* age? Same as your sister, right?"

"She's twenty six and, like my sister, you aren't touching her either."

"Ooh, he's jealous."

"Hardly," Joe scoffed, although Reid's remark hit close to the truth. "And we're just working on a book."

"Keep telling yourself that," Kyle said.

"Let's load up and clear out," Joe commanded, diverting the guys' attention. Soon they were back in the firehouse, and while Chris made lunch, Joe sat at his desk and began to tackle the never-ending stack of paperwork. His cell phone buzzed. Susie had sent him a text. "Laura's confirmed. Can Taylor do Friday? Say around three?"

Joe typed back, "Will try. Will let you know."

He leaned back in his chair. Unless the alarm sounded,

he could take a few minutes. He dialed her phone. "Hello?"

"Hey, it's Joe."

"Joe."

He liked the warmth he heard, as if she were smiling. "Can you do Friday at three for the first shoot?"

He heard a rustle, could picture her looking at her paper calendar. "Yes. That should be fine. I'm on call, but I don't think I'll have to work as I close Saturday night. Besides, Beth will want the shift. She and her husband are saving up for a house."

Joe squashed the tiny thrill. This wasn't a date. "Great. Do you want me to pick you up? Or meet you?"

"These are studio shots, right?"

"The first one is, yes."

"Okay, it's easier if we can use my mom's garage. I'm house sitting. I store my stuff there, and it's great light. I'll text you the address. You can forward it along."

"Okay."

"Oh, and I've scheduled your family photos for the start of next month. Your mother said you're off."

"If not, I will be," Joe confirmed. He lifted a pencil, twisted it in his free hand.

"Perfect. Anything else?"

Joe tightened his grip on his cell phone. Yes. There was more. She was the first female in a long time that made him consider risking rejection, made him consider dipping his toe in the dating pool. "No. Thanks again for helping me with this."

"No problem," Taylor said. She hesitated the briefest

of seconds, but he heard it. Felt it. "Bye Joe."

Joe swiveled his hand, pressing the power button and watching the screen go black. What would he have said? Hey, I told Reid he couldn't ask you out. I didn't like that he even thought about it. The guys think I should date more. Chris got engaged. I've thought of nothing but how I should have kissed you. Joe stuck the pencil back into the holder with a vicious shove.

"Did that pencil do something wrong?"

"Nah," Joe told Chris, who stood in the open doorway. "I assume lunch is ready?"

"Come and get it before Kyle eats it all. You know how he is with spaghetti."

Joe rose. "Spaghetti again?"

Chris shrugged. "It's all I can make. Boil noodles and open a jar of sauce. Bake the preseasoned bread at three fifty."

"You're pathetic."

"Which is why I'm marrying a woman who can cook." Chris tapped his forehead. "See, I'm thinking. She's also really good at—"

"No need for the details," Joe said.

"I was going to say baking. She dropped off a cake while we were out. Where was your mind, lieutenant? Oh those pink panties, I bet."

"Keep it up and you may not make it to that wedding," Joe threatened as they entered the common room. The aroma of simmering sauce and garlic bread permeated the space. "At least it smells good."

"Ye of little faith," Chris said, stepping aside so Joe, who was his superior, could go first.

As Joe grabbed a plate, he realized perhaps that that was the heart of the matter—faith.

He could rush into a burning building and take on a man in the boxing ring. But when it came to women, he was literally once burned and twice shy.

No amount of misguided faith would change that.

Chapter Seven

So this is where Taylor had grown up. Joe drove down the cul-de-sac directly across from Ursuline Academy and parked in the driveway of a ranch house in the middle of the block. As he exited, he heard the roar of the train that rumbled down the tracks directly behind her childhood home.

She opened the door as if she'd been waiting for him. "Hi."

"Hey," he said, drinking her in. Her ponytail swished, and he couldn't help notice the tank top that showcased her assets and the blue jean shorts that showed off long, shapely legs. Open-toe sandals revealed toenails painted hot pink. A dormant part of his libido stirred. "Can I get you anything? Soda? Iced tea? Lemonade? Beer? Water? My mom stocked up."

He knew exactly what he wanted from her, but said instead, "Ice water would be great." Remain professional, he chided himself, trying to ignore how tempting she was.

"No problem." Taylor moved with ease in the all-white cabinetry, stainless steel appliance kitchen, grabbing a glass and filling it from an automatic dispenser on the refrigerator. "You aren't allergic to cats, are you?"

As if on cue, the two Himalayans she'd told him about appeared. "Those are Yin and Yang." He arched an eyebrow and she laughed. "I know. My mom's unique that way. It's part of her charm. She's so quirky every winter she practiced her figure skating on the pond across the street until some school official finally put up a sign forbidding any skating. It was sad. The kids would also hold pick-up hockey games there."

"Did you go to Ursuline?"

"Kirkwood. Ursuline would have been convenient, but I was quite boy crazy and Kirkwood had a great journalism program, and that's where I fell in love with photography."

"Yearbook staff."

"Photo editor and proud to be a yerd." Her grin widened as she handed him the glass. "Yearbook nerd. Follow me. Garage is this way. I've got everything set up."

As Joe stepped into the garage, he saw she'd chosen a gray backdrop, which she'd rolled ten feet onto the concrete.

"Hello?"

"Back here," Joe answered. Two women came into view. Joe introduced them. "Taylor, this is Laura and her mother Amanda."

"Hi Taylor." Amanda reached out her hand.

An impish seven-year-old pointed to the backdrop. "Is that where I'm going to stand?"

"Why yes, it is." Taylor nodded and reached for her camera. Joe caught her by the shoulder, leaned, and whispered in her ear. He'd seen the shocked expression she'd quickly masked.

"Hey, you okay?"

No, she wasn't okay, Taylor thought. She'd never been one for surprises, and she'd assumed they were starting with Joe's sister, not this young child who'd clearly suffered a great deal. Taylor, admittedly shaken, leaned into Joe's shoulder, her face turned away from where Laura was chatting happily with her mother. That way they couldn't see her shock or the tears that threatened. She inhaled a comforting breath, drawing in his unique woodsy scent. He calmed her, she realized. "I thought we were starting with Susie."

"Laura's off for vacation, and she and her family are leaving for Maine. They'll be gone over a month, so I figured we needed to get this done."

She fiddled with the camera, regaining control. "She's so young."

"I'm sorry I didn't prepare you better."

Taylor didn't answer, but instead turned back to Laura. "You ready to be a model?"

"Yes!" Laura shouted, her enthusiasm contagious. "Models are beautiful."

"You are beautiful," Taylor said, meaning every word.

Laura's hazel eyes became saucers. "Really?"

"Absolutely. Now let's prove it." Taylor smiled at the girl whose wrinkled face revealed that she'd had multiple surgeries to repair horrific burns that traveled down one side of her face and down her neck. "The camera never lies, Laura, so all I'll need you to do is follow the directions."

Laura made a pose. "I'm good with directions."

"I can see you are."

Two hours later, once Laura and her mom had left, Taylor opened the refrigerator and withdrew two bottles of Schlafly's Pale Ale. She handed one to Joe and passed over an opener. "It's five o'clock somewhere."

"Here, by the looks of the microwave," Joe said, popping the top. "Good work today."

"Thanks." She drew down a long swallow. She'd thought weddings were draining. Those were a piece of cake compared to this. Several times, like when she'd photographed the newborns that night at the hospital, she'd bitten back tears.

Joe took a long drink and clinked his bottle to hers. "You were fantastic. Did you see how happy Laura was? While you were putting away your camera, Amanda told me how impressed she was."

"Good to know." He stood so close, mere inches away. Taylor's hand shook as she lifted the bottle again. "I thought I could handle this."

"You did. You made Laura feel beautiful. Special. Just like that mother in the hospital." He reached forward, tucked a loose strand of hair behind her ear. "You have a gift that way. That's why I asked you for your help. Why you are so perfect . . . for this project."

She'd heard that little pause, and her body liked the way his hand stroked the side of her cheek. She faced him. "Tell me it becomes easier."

"What?"

"Easier," she repeated, leaning her cheek into his hand.

His brow wrinkled. "The photos? You were great. Or are we talking about something else?"

She didn't even know. His touch had short-circuited her nervous system. Her emotions were all over the place. "She was so young."

"Hot grease. She pulled a frying pan off the stove, and it crashed down over her face. Today helped ease some of Amanda's guilt."

He set his beer on the counter and drew her into his arms. "Come here. You did great today. You gave Laura a gift. A beautiful gift."

A sniffle escaped her. "Then why am I crying? I don't cry, and I've cried more since meeting you than I did when I broke it off with Owen. Even when things were bad with him, I never cried."

"It's because you have a big heart."

"I just wish it was enough."

He tipped her head back. Locked his gaze onto hers. "It's more than enough."

"I wish I could believe it."

"Believe it." Gazes locked, she reached up to touch his face, feeling the emerging stubble. She slid her hand around the side of his neck and up into the dark strands he'd worn loose. Then she took what she needed. She encountered no resistance as she brought his mouth down to hers.

He tasted delicious. Like a slice of chocolate cake, only better. Lips pressed, lightened. Pressed again. He drew her closer and she angled her lips so the kiss could deepen. Sparks flew as his tongue found hers. Her eyes closed, tears banished as passion took their place. She curled her fingers, threading them further into his seductive hair. No wonder women loved long hair. Legolas. Aragorn. Thor. Stuff of fantasies, but with Joe, very real. And better. Oh, so much better. A mewling cry of pleasure escaped her as he plundered her mouth. Maybe it was his age. His experience. Finally, it was like in those romance novels she devoured. She'd never been kissed like this before, as if a kiss was a mutual possession.

He broke the connection to nibble his way down her neck, tracing a sensual line down to the scoop of her tank top. An ache began between her thighs and instinctively she pressed forward and up, her aching breasts searching. He used a hand to yank the garment and her bra down, bringing his mouth to her needy peak.

His tongue circled, and she arced toward his mouth, the wave of pleasure coursing through her so resplendent. He freed her other breast, lavishing attention on both peaks until her knees buckled from sheer pleasure as a tiny orgasm shot through her whole body and she shook. He recaptured her mouth, kissing her senseless. He didn't bother with the button, instead simply sliding fingers under the hem of her shorts and underwear until he found her soaked center. His kiss captured her moan as he rubbed a circle until she came hard and fast with ragged breath.

"Joe," she breathed, wanting—no, needing—to reciprocate, to feel him.

As she reached for the button on his jeans, it was like a bucket of cold water washed over Joe. What the hell was he doing? His hands pinned hers, stopping her from going further. "No," he told her between kisses. He pulled his mouth away. "No."

"But," she protested, her desirous eyes confused. Still, he kept her hands pinned. Part of him throbbed, for he wanted the release her touch promised. *But not here. Not like this*. Not when he hadn't been completely honest with her about his own scars. His mom had raised a respectful man, and he had to be one, not matter how much his body thought otherwise.

"We need to stop," he told her.

As reality intruded, Taylor crashed back to earth with a violent thump. "What? Why?" She winced. But how did you sound calm, cool, and collected after a man touched your most intimate spot, brought you to orgasm and then decided that continuing was a bad idea?

From hot to cold in two seconds flat meant her head warred with everything from rejection to regret to anger to unsatisfied desire. "I'm sorry," he said.

Anger won. "Don't you dare say that. Don't you dare tell me you hated that you led me on."

"I . . ."

She rounded on him. She hadn't given herself to anyone since Owen beyond a perfunctory good-night kiss. "I didn't need a hook-up."

"It's not a hook-up," he countered, stepping back. "Never. That's why I'm stopping." His arms crossed. "It's not you. It's me."

"I hate those words."

"I would never lie to you. We have to work together. The book." Clearly he was agitated. At a loss for words. A hand jerked through his hair, hair she'd fisted with abandon. "I don't regret what happened, but it was a mistake."

"That sounds like regret to me. Why are men always so complicated?"

"I . . ." He'd leaned against the cabinets, and he straightened and slid sideways, even further away. "Look at me. I'm hard as a rock. It's not that I don't want you."

"Then explain. Because I feel cheap."

He thrust his hands in his pockets. Took them out again. "That was never my intention. I have issues, okay? It seriously is me. Not you."

"What kind of issues? I don't understand." She could see the bulge. His body desired hers. "You're not dating someone, are you?"

He appeared horrified. "No."

"Then what is it?" She'd calmed somewhat.

He brushed back his hair again. "It's just wrong. . . . And I'm due at the gym. You are an awesome woman. If the circumstances were different . . ." his voice trailed off.

"Trust me, you deserve better. I'll call you."

And then he was out of the kitchen, unfinished beer sitting on the counter. She glanced out the window, watched his car back out of the driveway. She pounded her hand on the counter. What was it with men screwing with her head? Her high school boyfriend of six months had taken her virginity and then dumped her a week later. Then Owen had turned into a possessive, obsessive crazy person. Now Joe had told her he had issues. She chugged the rest of the bottle and resisted the urge to shatter it on the counter. Breaking things never helped, and that type of conflict resolution had been Owen's mojo.

Sensing something was wrong, Yin and Yang wove between her legs, their plaintive meows indicating they wanted to comfort her by providing themselves as objects for petting. She dumped Joe's beer and carried the rinsed bottles to the garage for recycling. She began to put the background away. So much for their sharing a moment.

She'd thrown herself at him and been tossed aside with a dumb excuse. She wouldn't make the same mistake again, and she certainly wouldn't ever embarrass herself this way again. No. Been there, done that.

Her phone buzzed and she answered. "Hey Taylor," her manager, John, said. "Can you work tonight? Lisa's out sick."

Taylor's answer was instantaneous. Stay home and wallow or get out and earn some money. "Absolutely," she told him. "I'll be right in."

***

"So how did the shoot go?" Susie asked the next day, her legs bending. She pulled abreast with him on the climbing wall.

"Fine," Joe said. He craned his neck, assessing the next rock protrusions. The wall they were on was forty-five feet high, and they were two thirds of the way up.

"Just 'fine'?" She grappled the next outcropping, pulled herself upward. The spotter below took the slack out of her line. "Amanda called me gushing."

"Taylor did a great job." He yanked himself upward. After leaving Taylor, he'd gone to the gym, gone two rounds with a worthy opponent to work out his frustrations.

"So what's the problem?" Susie hung there, waiting for him to catch up. "Something's wrong. I can tell."

"I'm fine. I lost last night's fight."

"You never lose."

"He got in a lucky shot. I'm a bit sore, that's all. Didn't block as well as I should have."

"Now, I know something's wrong," Susie called as he passed her by. "Nothing ever gets by you." She hauled herself upward. "I'm going to be too big for this soon. So tell me, what's got you in a state?"

"Nothing. I am not in a state." His foot slipped, but he caught himself before he swung off the wall and into empty space.

"You're lying, and you never lie, so it's obvious when

you do. You forget I know you. Maybe it's because of what happened when we were kids."

"Don't remind me."

She ignored him. "Because of it, we have a bond. A close friendship beyond being related. Which means you owe me the truth."

"Fine," he grumbled. He loved all his brothers and sisters, but Susie was correct. He was closer to her than the others.

"Spill," she demanded as she came level again. She drilled him with the look she'd perfected from their mother.

"I kissed her."

"Who?" Her eyes widened a millisecond later as she figured it out. "No way!"

He studied the next rock outcropping.

"You didn't! I could tell you liked her at the picnic, but . . ." Susie, forgetting where she was, covered her mouth with her hand, and lost her balance. She swung out into the air. "Damn! You are so going to tell me everything." Joe climbed further away from where she dangled. "You have to come down sometime," Susie warned as the spotter below began to lower her to the ground. "I'll be waiting."

"We'll see," Joe called after her, but oddly, unburdening himself felt decent. He'd made a mistake, and Susie would help him deal with it. They shared the same experiences, the same love and loss. Although she'd found Parker.

Susie was drinking a strawberry banana smoothie

from the juice bar when he caught up with her. "So, this kiss."

"Yeah. About that. It was a mistake."

Susie winced. "Did you say that to her? Please tell me you didn't say that to her."

He gritted his teeth. *Busted.* He gave a sad chuckle. "You know I'm not good with women. All looks, no follow-through."

"Joe."

He waved over the bartender, ordered a G2. Drained half of it. "Maybe you should take over this project."

"Joe." The way she sighed his name revealed marked resignation. He knew she was frustrated with him. "You have to get back out there. You can't hide out the first time being with some woman scares you."

"There's nothing wrong with being a bachelor."

"Except that you don't want to be."

"Do this for me," he asked, avoiding addressing that particular issue. "Take over the book. I can learn how to take photos some other way."

She took a sip of her smoothie. "I'm the next one anyway. I need to call Taylor to set it up. I'll talk to her."

"Thanks," Joe said, finishing the last of his orange-flavored drink.

"You know she will be there for the family shoot."

Joe stood up and gave his sister a peck on the forehead. "But then we won't be alone, and it's weeks away. I've got to run. Literally. I'm off to do ten miles."

She waved him away, turned and stared at the remains

of her smoothie. Drummed her fingers on the table. Her oldest brother was so pig-headed. So darn stubborn, almost to a fault. Well, she'd promised to talk to Taylor, but she hadn't promised to say what Joe wanted her to say. Splitting hairs, but in the Marino family, something she'd learned to do well.

She tugged her cell phone out of her pocket, pressed a button she'd programmed into speed dial. "Hey," she said the moment her mother answered. "We've got a problem."

***

"Thank you for agreeing to do this," Susie said. "And so quickly."

Taylor smiled as Susie posed against the background. "Well, my mom's not back yet. Seems she and her friend got lost on the way back from Topeka."

"Lost?" Susie wore a silver-sequined designer mini that showcased her rounding figure. Marci had stopped by to do Susie's hair and makeup. Susie was beautiful, despite the wrinkled skin that covered toned legs and parts of her arms.

"Well, what was to be a two-day trip has turned into a week-long adventure. They had to see the sights in Topeka, of course."

"Of course." Susie nodded, catching Taylor's sarcasm.

"And then they made it as far as Kansas City and they're still there, staying at some hotel on the Plaza. It's all a con to get me to move back in here, I'm sure."

"Well, it's a nice place. I had to share a room growing up."

"There is that. I did have my own space. Now angle your shoulder more. Yes, like that." Taylor pressed the shutter and shot a few more frames. "Okay, that's a wrap."

Susie looked like a kid in the candy store. "So I can see them?"

Taylor laughed. "Absolutely. Even with the fan, it's getting hot out here, so let's go inside and we can look at them on my computer. Could I get you something to drink?"

"Water is fine." Taylor smiled and shook her head. "What?" Susie asked.

"You and Joe. My mom fully stocks this fridge so it looks like the beverage aisle at Dierberg's, and that's all he wanted too."

"We're simple people," Susie said. "My parents weren't big on sugary sweets. Not with six kids in the house. My mom even kept the real Oreos hidden in a closet in her bedroom. We got the store-brand sandwich cremes. Trust me, you can taste the difference. To this day I refuse to let them in my house."

"Ouch," Taylor said, reaching into a cabinet and bringing out a blue package. "That is cruel because I've bought those and you're right, they are awful. Here, my mom buys the real thing. Let me get us some water."

Water and Oreos in hand, they sat at the breakfast bar as Taylor took the SD card out of her camera and slid it into a slot on her Mac. She then opened up all the photos.

"Now remember, they aren't retouched. I'll lighten, tweak, and work some digital magic. But they are fabulous. See?"

As Taylor began to scroll through, her phone rang. "Just press the arrow key," she told Susie as she grabbed her cell and stood.

"Hello?"

"Taylor, it's Virginia. I've decided to host a little dinner party at my house to introduce the calendar guys to the media, and as the photographer, I want you to be there. Thursday night at five. I'm on Upper Ladue Road. Number . . ."

Taylor grabbed a pen and pad of paper from the urn her mother kept on the counter. She scribbled down the information. "I'll be there."

"Perfect. And how is your new project coming?"

"The Burns Recovered Support Group book? It's going great. I'm two shoots in."

"Excellent. Well, I think our calendar will be an annual project, so pencil us in for next year. See you Thursday. Semi-formal. Not black tie. We'll save that for the ball."

Taylor hung up. "Looks like I'm going to a cocktail party slash dinner."

Susie glanced up. "Sounds fancy."

"It's to promote the calendar." She leaned against the bar stool back. "I assume Joe will be there."

"Excellent. Then you can work things out."

Taylor frowned. "I didn't realize there were things to work out."

Susie gestured to the computer. "These are really good,

by the way. I've never seen myself look so good, and I loved Laura's shots."

"Thanks." The compliment warmed.

"Now that we have all the shoots arranged, it'll go pretty quickly."

"It should." Taylor devoured an Oreo, her number-one comfort food.

"But that doesn't address the problem," Susie continued.

"What problem?" Taylor inhaled another one.

"The problem of my brother. Both of you keep saying the same things."

"I don't understand." Taylor reached for her water. Wished she'd gotten a big glass of milk instead.

Eyes similar to Joe's pinned her. "Do you like him?"

Taylor sputtered mid-sip and then hiccupped. "What?"

Susie didn't falter. "I asked, do you like him?"

"That's not an appropriate question."

Susie wasn't put off. "Of course it is. He kissed you and then said it was a mistake. I'd say, given all the work we all have to do, you both need to work things out. Wouldn't you agree?"

Taylor leaned back. To heck with water or milk. If she didn't have to work at five, she'd grab a beer out of the fridge. "I can't believe he told you we'd kissed."

"I'm sure he can't believe he kissed you. Despite how sexy my brother is, well, he's awkward with women."

"This is crazy. We're professional colleagues," Taylor

protested.

"Did you know what I did before I married Parker?"

Taylor shook her head. "No."

"Worked as an administrative assistant to the battalion chief. Parker went after me like a house on fire. He made me feel special, and I didn't feel I deserved him. I mean, look at me."

"You're beautiful."

"But I didn't feel that way. Who could love this?" She gestured to her arms and legs. "Kids teased me, or they whispered behind my back. I was the freak. Then one day, I didn't care anymore. You met Laura. I've never met a braver little girl. Even in the heat of summer, I can try to cover up. She has to literally face the world and smile through the scars."

"I cried. I think that's why he kissed me."

"Joe's a huge helper, but he doesn't kiss out of pity."

"Good to know." Taylor grabbed another cookie.

Susie placed a reassuring hand on her arm. "You have a big heart. Joe told me about your work with babies. I couldn't do that. I can't imagine. It's why Joe knew you were perfect for this project and why I know you're perfect for him."

Taylor didn't know what to make of that. "Really, I—"

"Do you like him?" Susie asked, interrupting.

"What does that have to do with anything?"

"Everything, I'd say," Susie countered.

"This isn't high school. It's not that simple. We don't really know each other. Sure, he's sexy as sin. When he stands near me, I get butterflies. But the physical attraction doesn't mean anything. It can actually be downright scary. And this is a really odd conversation to be having."

"If you think *I'm* bad, wait until my mother starts in on you."

"Maybe I should reconsider doing your family's photos."

"Don't you dare." Susie laughed before her expression intensified. "And I'm serious. Don't you dare."

"I'll finish what I started. Just do not try to make a love connection between me and Joe."

"Actually, that's up to both of you. And while I'd love to see him happy, there's something else I want you to do instead."

"Sounds ominous."

Susie fingered her water glass in a gesture similar to Joe's. "Well, it will be difficult. I want you to add one more person to the book."

Taylor shrugged. Ate another Oreo. "That doesn't sound too scary. But I thought everyone who was interested signed up at one of your meetings."

"Well, technically yes. That's why you'll have to convince this one. It's the reason I asked if you liked Joe. You'll need his help."

"He's been helping. I'm sure we can put aside our differences, and our desires, to get the job done."

"For these specific pictures, you will need Joe's full cooperation. He's not going to want to do them. But he must."

Taylor was confused. "Why not?"

"Because it's him. He's the one you must photograph. Haven't you noticed that he's always covered from his waist down? Even when he boxes, he's pretty much covered up. He hates having his legs exposed. Hates it."

Taylor's fingers stilled, and the water from the faucet began overflowing the glass. Her mouth dropped. "Joe is scarred?"

"Yes." Susie nodded. "I wasn't the only one injured that day. I want Joe in the book. I want you to help him to feel whole again, as you did for me and for Laura." Susie hit the arrow to display another picture. "Look how good I look. It's like a celebration that being burned didn't keep me from being whole. He deserves to feel that way too, don't you think?"

"I didn't realize he'd been burned. He told me he tried to save you."

"He did. In more ways than one. He needs to be in this book as much as I do, as much as Laura and the others. I've asked him, but he won't listen to me and I no longer have anything to hold over his head. If I did, I'd bribe him. Blackmail him. I'm not above that." Her intense expression indicated how serious she was.

Taylor turned off the water. Sipped until the volume was at a safe level. Wiped the glass with a paper towel. "So you expect *me* to ask? I have even less power over him. I doubt I can convince him."

Joe was a proud man—Taylor could tell that from day one. He was a burn survivor. Now his cocky behavior at the photo shoot made sense. Now his rejection—his declaration that they'd made a mistake—made sense. He didn't want her to see his flaws, much less let her know he had them. "He's not going to be happy I know his secret. He's going to be even less happy that you . . . I . . . we want to put him in the book."

Susie's gaze sharpened. "Oh, he's going to hate every minute. But I'll leave solving that little problem up to you."

"Great. Is this when I say, gee thanks?" But she'd do it, Taylor knew. Her nature to help people couldn't do less.

Susie lifted her glass and held it in a toast. "You know, if nothing else, I think you and I are going to be good friends."

Taylor clinked her glass to Susie's. "To friendship. Because if your brother reacts the way I predict he will, I'm going to need all the friends I can get."

Chapter Eight

As Taylor's black Chevy Cobalt crept up Upper Ladue Road, she felt like she stuck out like a sore thumb. The mansions on this block all sat on at least two acres and started at $2.5 million. She'd definitely entered the high-rent district, where the yearly real estate taxes totaled more than an experienced teacher made in a year.

She found the driveway, turned in, and rattled across a wooden bridge. After a short jaunt under a canopy of thick trees, she gasped as the massive white stone structure came into view. Designed like an English country manor, she counted six chimneys. A guy in a red vest directed her forward, then opened her car door and gave her a ticket. "I'll park it, miss."

"Oh, okay," Taylor said as he assisted her from the car. She tugged the hem of her strapless dress before it rode up her thighs and embarrassed her, as the Cobalt did when it was whisked away and parked next to a Bentley.

She tucked the ticket into her satin wristlet, which,

like the strapless peach chiffon Alice and Olivia dress, came from the designer resale shop. Another valet showed her to the side door. When she stepped in, a waiter handed her a glass of champagne and directed her to the great room where everyone mingled.

"Taylor," Virginia said, giving her air kisses. "So glad you could come. Let me introduce you to my husband, Ted. Ted, this is Taylor, the photographer I told you about."

"Nice to meet you," Taylor said, shaking his hand. Then Virginia drew her off to meet someone else. And then someone else, until Virginia said, "Don't look now, but there's your man."

Taylor swiveled her head and hiccupped. She'd seen Joe in his turnout gear, in a pink T-shirt and jeans, and in his white polo shirt. Tonight he wore a dark blue suit coat, a tailored pinstripe shirt, and dress pants. He'd left his brown hair loose, giving him a "Fashion Rocks," red carpet vibe. Women surrounded him, and he managed them all easily.

"Mmm hmm," Virginia said. "He's going to be a popular one. He'll sell lots of calendars."

"There are eleven other months," Taylor pointed out.

"And all equally as hot. But there's something about him, wouldn't you say?"

She would say, but Taylor simply nodded as Virginia patted her arm and moved to speak with someone else. Taylor again glanced at Joe, who was still surrounded. She accepted something from the appetizer tray a roving waiter offered as she made brief conversation with cop Jack Donovan, Mr. December. Then, with a bite of food and half a glass of champagne under her belt, she joined the queue surrounding Mr. September.

"So what's the scariest fire you've ever been in?" a fortysomething woman asked. A huge diamond winked on her ring finger as she took another sip of champagne.

"We take all of them seriously," Joe evaded.

"Is it like *Chicago Fire*?" another woman asked. She leaned a little too close to Joe for Taylor's liking. "I love that TV show."

"The reality is—" Joe began.

"Probably not as exciting as Hollywood makes it seem," Taylor inserted with a wide smile. She shoved her right hand forward. "I'm Taylor Krebs. The photographer. Weren't you there when we picked out the photos?"

The woman smiled, pleased Taylor had remembered. "Why yes, I was. You did a wonderful job."

"She was very professional," Joe inserted, never losing his smile. "My family has hired her to do our family portraits."

"Why, that's wonderful," another woman said. "I always thought you had to go to the studio for that. But I guess wedding photographers travel."

"Exactly," Taylor said.

"You'll have to give me your business card."

Taylor extracted one, and the woman put it in her wristlet. At that moment, Virginia tapped a knife on her champagne glass, made a short speech, and then told everyone to head into the dining room where caterers had a buffet set up. "Sit anywhere," she offered.

"Shall we?" Joe said. He motioned toward the food.

"What, you'd like me to join you?"

He offered her his arm. "Isn't that why you came over here? I'm sure after a photo session with my sister, you have plenty to say to me."

"Did she tell you what we discussed?"

Joe's head shook. "No. Said I'd have to ask you. Said that if you wanted to tell me, you would."

Taylor should have known. "Well, isn't she the slippery one?"

"That's one word for it. Much milder than I'd use as I've known her all my life."

"Drove you crazy I'm sure."

"You could say that," Joe admitted. "But then she does most days."

They approached the buffet. "This looks positively delicious."

She began to fill her plate with chicken breast in sauce, sliced roast beef, new potatoes, almond-garnished green beans, and a buttery dinner roll. She skipped the kale and lettuce salad, although Joe added it to his plate.

"There's a table outside," Joe said, and she followed him onto the terrace. Being a nice night, others had the same idea, and diners occupied most of the ten or so tables that surrounded a beautifully landscaped, inground pool. Joe set his plate down and pulled out a chair.

"Why thank you," she said as she sat.

"My mother raised a gentleman. And that dress is lovely." He pushed her in.

"Thank you again. You're scaring me, being on your best behavior."

"Well, we didn't part on the best of terms. I made a bit of an ass of myself."

"A bit of an understatement." She forked some potatoes into her mouth. "Mmm. This is so good. Who knew new potatoes could be gourmet? I could get used to how the other half live."

He shook his head, the hair swishing. "Not me. It's too much. And did you see all that wallpaper in the dining room? It looks like a decorator vomited flowers everywhere. Not my taste at all."

"You wouldn't want a place like this?"

"Too big. Too ostentatious. Even if I could live in a house like this, I don't think I would. I bet they never go into half the rooms."

They laughed at that, ate a few more bites until a couple approached.

"Do you mind if we join you?"

"No, please do." Joe indicated the two empty chairs and the couple sat down.

"I'm Melanie and this is my husband Dean. Virginia's my mom. My brother is Stuart. He's the lawyer who took over after my dad retired."

"That's Joe and I'm Taylor."

"The photographer." Melanie faced Joe. "And you're one of the months."

"Yes," Joe answered.

"Thank you so much for volunteering to be in the calendar. It's for such a good cause. So how long have you been dating?" Melanie asked.

"Uh, we aren't—"

"Since we met on the calendar shoot." Joe cut Taylor off and she coughed while chewing a piece of chicken. He thumped her on the back. "Good thing I'm trained in saving people, right honey?"

Everyone chuckled, and Taylor drank more champagne. "You okay dear?" he asked with a warning expression that indicated he'd explain later. Considering his earlier rejection when they'd started to be intimate, he'd better. He'd pay for this stunt later. Taylor touched her throat. "Thanks honey."

"So sweet," Melanie said, grabbing Dean's hand.

"Yep." Joe grabbed Taylor's hand and kissed the back of it. "I treat her like a princess."

"So sweet," Melanie gushed again.

"That he is." Taylor removed her hand, picked up her knife, and shoved it into the roast beef before she found another target.

The foursome began to eat, limiting conversation to safer topics like Cardinals baseball. Then Melanie and Dean finished and stood to leave. "It was so nice meeting you," Melanie said.

Taylor turned on Joe the moment the couple was out of earshot. "Why did you do that?"

"What?" Joe asked.

"Tell them we were dating?"

"Because it seemed easier than answering all their ensuing questions, and I've already been approached like three times. I wanted a shield."

"But we're not dating."

"So? Sometimes the path of least resistance is the easiest one. If they think I'm with you, no one will play matchmaker."

"For someone who swears he never lies, you let them believe something that wasn't true. For someone who helps, I can't believe you did that."

"I said I would never lie to you and I haven't. What I said to them was harmless. We can be broken up by the time we leave tonight. Virginia and her family are do-gooders out to help the world, as this shindig clearly shows. If we weren't already dating, I'm sure they'd be figuring out some other way to get us to date, or if not, all the other matchmakers are going to try to have me hitched by the time I reach my car. I get enough of that from my mom. So I beat them to the punch."

She shook her head. "But now they're working under false impressions."

"Sometimes playing along is the best response in my line of work. If you're in a car accident or a fire, you want your first responder to give you hope, even if there is none. You always tell people it's going to be fine, that you'll take care of them. And you do, no matter what."

"Okay," Taylor said slowly, contemplating the situations he'd been in. "That makes sense."

"I try to be honest to a core, so it's a hard thing to rationalize. Sometimes it doesn't even make sense. I just didn't want to be bothered tonight answering a lot of unnecessary questions, and I certainly don't want to be seen as single and eligible."

"Why did you tell your sister about our kiss?"

He didn't deny it. "Because she's a bulldog with endless questions. Doing so was probably a mistake."

She arched an eyebrow. "You seem to be making a lot of those lately."

"Yeah, I guess so." He fingered the champagne flute stem. "Speaking of being completely honest, I should tell you that I'm not good with relationships. They're not my strong suit. Not even close." He lifted the glass to his lips. Drained it. "We've clearly got some physical chemistry, but I don't want to be ruled by my desires. I did that once with terrible results."

She wondered what he meant, but he didn't elaborate, just kept speaking with firm conviction.

"I can't make those types of mistakes ever again, and with you, I'm tempted. Far too much."

The admission came at a high cost, she knew. His sense of morality was his biggest strength, but also his biggest flaw.

"So what do we do? Because I'm attracted to you too," she said, choosing to be honest. After all, to work together they did have to sort through this. Find resolution.

"I don't know." Another honest answer.

"Maybe we should spend time together. We have to

anyway," she suggested. "After all, we're dating now," she added, trying to make a joke.

Before Joe could respond, Virginia approached their table.

"Look at you two lovebirds. Melanie told me you were out here. See, Taylor, I told you so. I'm always right."

Taylor resisted the urge to slide beneath the table. Joe should have considered Virginia's daughter would spread the news. "Joe, Chief Winchester tells me you're boxing in the tournament this Saturday."

Joe nodded. "Yes."

Taylor hadn't known Joe's chief was there, although she'd learned tonight that to Virginia a small dinner party meant over sixty people. She'd met maybe a third of the guests.

"So, you'll be there as well, right, Taylor?" Virginia asked.

"Uh." She looked helplessly at Joe.

"Of course you have to be there," Virginia insisted. "What type of a girlfriend would you be if you weren't supporting your man during his match?"

What was that about telling a fib? That it just kept growing and growing? "I thought the tickets were all sold out."

Virginia waved a hand. "That's no problem. I have plenty of extra. I'm on the BackStoppers board of directors."

Of course she was. Virginia seemed to be in charge of everything St. Louis related.

"This is an important matchup. If Joe wins, he'll compete in the annual Guns 'N Hoses the night before Thanksgiving. You know that's one of the biggest fundraisers for the BackStoppers."

Taylor realized she'd forgotten to Google it. She'd meant to after he'd told her that night at Dressel's, but then she'd promptly gotten busy with the calendar photos.

"I don't want to distract him." And the idea of watching men hit each other, even with boxing gloves, simply didn't sound appealing. She just hadn't wanted to tell him that night.

Virginia didn't seem to notice her discomfort. "You can go with me and Ted. We'd love to have you as our guest. We'll keep you sequestered away until after Joe's match."

"Then it's settled," Joe said, giving Taylor a grin that once again proved he was firmly in control even though she felt like she was spiraling. "Although, I do have to work at seven the next morning."

"We'll take it easy that night," Taylor told him. He gave her another wicked smile.

"Besides, honey, maybe boxing could be a good subject for your project." An eyebrow arched, daring her.

A project for which she still didn't have approval. "Oh, aren't the two of you cute," Virginia gushed. "Taylor, call me tomorrow so we can make a plan. You met Melanie and Dean, so perhaps you'd love to join us for dinner beforehand as well."

Taylor's eyes widened. The hiccups threatened. "I . . ."

"She'd love to," Joe replied, sending her a sharp glance. "Wouldn't you dear?"

She was going to kill him later. Positively kill him. "Um, okay."

"Perfect. I love it when a plan comes together. We'll talk tomorrow." Virginia beamed as she moved away.

Taylor sat back against the chair with a thump. "What did you think you were doing?"

"Getting you into Virginia's good graces. She's obviously looking for a protégée and you're it."

"Well, I doubt you saw that coming when you said we were dating."

"Chalk up another mistake on my part," Joe said. "But if it helps you, I'll play along."

Taylor shook her head. "I don't even like boxing."

"Have you ever been to a boxing match?"

She shook her head and he frowned.

"You had no idea what Guns 'N Hoses was."

"Still don't," she admitted.

"You forgot to Google."

"Guilty. I've seen *Rocky*. Well, parts of it anyway."

"It's honestly a lot different. So you're judging something you've never even experienced. Bit stereotypical, wouldn't you say?"

"I don't even know why you'd do it. Is it the testosterone? The thrill?"

"I'm a champ. It's primal. It's for charity. It helps me stay in shape, and that helps me rescue people."

A roving waiter came by offering more champagne.

Taylor took at glass. Her hand shook slightly.

"You should be flattered," Joe told her. "Virginia has taken a huge interest in you. She'll launch you big time if you let her. You do want that, don't you?"

"Yes. I think so." She wasn't sure of anything anymore. He'd turned her inside out. Her feelings changed rapid-fire when he was around."

"Well, it's all networking. You don't get here"—he gestured at the professionally manicured landscaping— "without knowing the right people. Bring your camera. Have some fun with it. Maybe your professor will finally cut you a break. When do you meet with him?"

"Soon. He took a brief trip. Will your family be there?"

"At Guns 'N Hoses, yes. Susie and Parker go as well as mom and dad and a few cousins. This match is in a smaller venue. They probably won't come to this, and I wouldn't expect them to with all the stuff they have going. Guns 'N Hoses is at the Enterprise Center. It's a big deal. For me, this is just practice."

She knew the Enterprise Center hosted professional hockey and concerts seated a little over nineteen thousand people. "Wow. I didn't know boxing was that big in St. Louis."

"Boxing and mixed martial arts. Fifteen three-round bouts."

She swallowed more bubbly. "What have you gotten me into?"

"Me? May I remind you that you kissed me first. You

put your hands in my hair and brought my head down and—"

"Yes," she interrupted quickly. The picture was still vivid, and she still really liked his hair. "But tonight you told people we were dating."

He grinned. Turned on the persuasion. "I guess that makes us even. I'm sure you'll survive one event. And if you hate boxing, then I'll concede the point, say you're right and I was wrong."

"The chance of hearing you say you were wrong makes it worth my while," she admitted.

He chuckled. "I'm sure you'll love it."

"Doubtful, but I'm in for a penny now and I'll give it a fair shake. And I'll bring my camera."

"See, I knew you couldn't resist the Marino charm." That wicked grin widened. The man was pure temptation.

She arched an eyebrow. "Charm . . . really? That's what it is?"

Those blue-gray-greens twinkled. "Of course."

"I'm not sure that's what just happened, but I'll let you believe otherwise. It's easier that way."

He raised his empty glass to her. "Touché."

Taylor couldn't help but smile. Bantering and verbally sparring with Joe was invigorating, and oddly a great time.

She could help him, she realized, like she helped the mothers who'd lost their children. Her father's words had been a part of her philosophy for years—she was to help everyone she could, and as long as she tried, as long as she'd done her best, it would be enough.

In Joe's case, she understood now why he couldn't let himself have her, why he held himself in such close check any time they were together. The photos would be therapy. Not pity, for Joe wouldn't suffer any of that, but instead a way for him to see himself as beautiful, to let the real Joe—the deep one that hid behind the Marino charm—to let the real Joe out once and for all. She could at least give him that gift. Her father would have wanted it that way.

Chapter Nine

"I had no idea boxing was such a big deal," Taylor marveled as she entered Chaifetz Arena, which was located on the St. Louis University campus. The venue could hold over ten thousand, and almost all the seats were full. The boxing match that served as one of the precursors to the November BackStoppers event hummed with a vibrant, tangible energy.

"A championship fight can earn over one hundred million just in Pay-Per-View revenue," Ted Barker told Taylor. "Floyd Mayweather made one hundred five million one year."

"Wow," Taylor said. "I never would have guessed. People really pay to watch the matches?"

"Yes. It's like buying an On Demand movie." Ted began to pass out wristbands. "We have a suite, but we can also be down on the floor. That's what these are for." They all snapped on the red plastic wristbands.

"Thanks so much for adding me," Marci said, her eyes

wide with excitement. "You sure I can't pay you for the ticket?"

"Of course not. The more the merrier, dear," Virginia said. "Shall we head to the suite?" She, her daughter, and her son-in-law led the way.

"I can't believe this," Marci whispered to Taylor as a personal attendant greeted them when they entered the suite. "Look at this."

"I am." Taylor's own eyes widened. Televisions hanging on cream-colored walls kept them appraised of the action down on the floor. Comfortable stuffed armchairs surrounded small tables, and the buffet table held an array of everything from chicken wings to popcorn. "Is the beer free?"

Taylor laughed. "It's all inclusive. As I'm driving, have at it."

"I think I will." Marci made a beeline for the bar.

Taylor sat in one of the chairs and picked up the program. Joe was one of the earlier bouts, and thanks to Virginia, she had a full-access pass to take photos. She lifted her camera out of the bag, made some adjustments, and took a few test shots. Aside from the Barker clan, there were ten other people in the suite. She recognized a few of them from the dinner party.

Marci came back with a clear plastic cup emblazoned with the Bud Light logo. "Do you know much these regularly cost? These people must be loaded."

Taylor didn't confirm or deny. "I want to take some pictures. Come with?"

"No, I'll hang out here for a bit. I'll text you if I'm bored."

Taylor nodded, slipped on her laminated pass, and made sure her wristband was secure. The boxers were staging in the various locker rooms, which was where she saw Joe. He wore below-the-knee, synthetic satin shorts with a wide, white waistband emblazoned with a Maltese cross that matched the one inked on his wrist, and custom above-the-ankle shoes and red and white socks that reached the hem of his bright red shorts. Currently he was shirtless.

Still unseen, she took his picture. He appeared lost in his own world, a Joe she hadn't seen before. He laced his black boxing boots, unlaced them, and laced them again. He'd pulled his hair back into a ponytail. He'd shaved—no evening shadow here.

"Hey, you can't—" She held up the plastic pass and the person fell quiet, went back to whatever he had been doing. She brought the viewfinder to her eye, peered through. It always amazed her how the camera allowed her to see things the naked eye couldn't. Like the way the harsh fluorescent lights brought out the lighter brown highlights infused in his black hair. His brow creased, his eyebrows knit together. She could almost see the wheels turn inside his head, as if working his way through the logistics of the upcoming bout. She adjusted the exposure to blur the background, filled the frame, and pressed the shutter, freezing Joe for eternity—or at least until she hit delete.

Joe hadn't seen her yet, and as his trainer approached, she used the opportunity to take more photos. He smiled, which lit up his entire face. There was something in that honest, real smile, something in the way his lips moved, that drew her. Created a pang inside her. Told her that she was in over her head.

She was already creating fantasies. Imagined his lips on hers again. Wondered what a real relationship would be like. Pretty typical female behavior, wasn't it? Didn't all women size up a guy to his potential? Taylor certainly wasn't looking for Mr. Right Now. But Mr. Right? Her camera whirred as she took more shots.

A cheer went up from a group of men watching a TV monitor. They must have liked the outcome of the bout, and she shot their jubilant reactions. Joe's head came around, and his gaze found her. His eyes widened, and he stood. Came over. "Hi."

"Hey." The camera strap rested next to the photo-pass lanyard. She let the camera dangle. "Virginia got me all-access. Thought I'd make use of it."

"Can I see the photos?"

"I don't want to distract you or interrupt your routine."

He took the camera off her neck, and the strap tickled. "You won't. I'm not that superstitious aside from wearing my lucky socks." He pointed to a pair of red socks that looked rather ordinary. "Show me. It'll give me a break. The waiting is the hardest part. If you think about things too long, you can psyche yourself out."

He began flipping through the images. "There's a lot of me."

The words rushed out. "I find you fascinating."

"Which is probably more frightening than the guy I'm about to face," Joe admitted. "I've beaten him twice. I'll get him the third time tonight. No worries. I'm in even better shape now than I was last year. Where will you be afterwards?"

She named the suite. "Okay, I'll shower and come up when I'm done. You going down on the floor?"

"I'm not really sure I want to be close enough to watch sweat fly."

"Makes for some good action shots." He draped the camera back over her neck and lifted her loose hair so the strap went against her neck. He twisted a curl before letting a strand bounce. "I'm up next."

"I should probably get back to the suite."

He pointed. "You've got the band. Go ringside."

She hesitated. "I don't want to distract you."

"You already do that."

A thrill mixed with worry. "Then I shouldn't—"

He put his fingers on her arm. The touch reassured. Soothed. "Once I'm in the ring, everything else fades to background noise. So don't worry. You won't destroy my concentration. You can do that after I win."

"If you win," she shot back, feeling more comfortable in the back-and-forth banter she was used to exchanging with him.

"Oh, I will. You can count on that."

"Joe, you're on deck in five."

"Gotta go. Need my gloves." He leaned over and

kissed her cheek, lingering for a second longer than necessary. "See you later."

Her cheek tingled, watching him as he disappeared into the bowels of the locker room. She snapped a few more pictures, then made her way ringside. There, during the lull between matches, she found Ted and his son-in-law in their front row seats.

"Come to join us for Joe's match?" Dean shouted over the blaring music.

"Yes," she shouted back. She adjusted her camera, took more shots. "This is fascinating."

Ted leaned forward so he didn't have to yell. "Joe's favored to win."

"Just saw him. He says he's ready."

"Have you watched him box before?"

"No. Honestly, I don't even know what happens. He wins if he knocks him out?"

"There's more to it than that," Ted explained. "The judge will count the power punches and jabs for an overall total.. Light punches with no force aren't counted. Then there's—"

She held up a hand. "I have no idea what you're talking about."

Dean laughed with her. "Melanie doesn't either, which is why she's upstairs." The music ended abruptly as the announcer stepped back into the ring. "Ladies and gentlemen," he began, but Taylor barely heard him. Her full attention was on the man waiting to climb into the ring. Joe's challenger entered first, circled the ring to adoring cheers.

Then the announcer called out ". . . five-time undefeated BackStoppers champion, Joe Marino . . ."

Joe stripped off his robe, revealing a red and white sleeveless boxing shirt tucked into his waistband. Like the gloves, he'd added it after they'd parted. Like a phoenix, he rose the four feet to the climb through the ropes, and as he commanded the ring, Taylor added her screams to those of the audience. The energy was electrifying. He made a circle around the twenty-three-foot square, and she lifted her camera, catching his self-assurance and his predatory prowl. He was primal. Male. Magnificent. Dominant.

The ladies in the audience clearly loved him, and the men respected him, for the crowd chanted "Joe. Joe." He was their rock star, their beloved champ.

The referee called the boxers into the center of the ring, spoke to them, and then gestured them back to their respective corners. Standing on the area outside the ropes, Joe's coach gave him last-minute instructions and helped him slide on the red protective headgear. Then Joe was on his feet and the bell rang. As the two men crossed the canvas, Taylor held her breath.

She knew none of the mechanics, couldn't tell an uppercut from a jab, but as Joe and his challenger engaged, the type of moves became irrelevant. Joe was the red Rock 'Em Sock 'Em Robot. He landed punch after punch in a fury, and from the seats on the floor she could hear every *swack* and *flapp* as the gloves connected with skin or the protective headgear. To her, three minutes seemed to fly.

The bell rang and Joe headed back to the corner, where he sat on his stool.

"He won that round," Dean said.

"Yes," Ted confirmed.

Habit had her lifting her camera and shooting nonstop as coaches wiped sweat while Joe took a quick drink. His trainer retied his hair, the one-minute break almost over.

"Boxing is all about leg strength," Ted told her. "To train, they run, they do sit-ups."

"He does marathons."

No wonder why Joe loved this sport. His burned legs might appear weak, but they were his key to victory.

"I did a few fights in my days. Back before the real world intruded and I gave it up after college. Your legs allow you to be grounded. Power comes up from the ground."

Power comes from the ground. Taylor could see how Joe would need that, how he'd determined to be strong so he could save others as he hadn't saved his sister.

A woman in a sequined dress and high heels paraded around the ring carrying a Round Two sign. The bell sounded as she left the ring.

Taylor adjusted the zoom, allowing her to focus close on Joe's face. His gaze rested on his opponent, nothing else mattered. The intensity overpowered her, and Taylor shivered. Then she pressed the shutter, tracking his movements as he landed the first punch; she shot through the entire three-minute round, which Joe won as well.

Muscles bulged, sweat gleamed. He hadn't tired, but she could tell he'd faded somewhat. So had his opponent. The bell sounded.

"One more," Ted said. "He's doing great. Unless he gets knocked out, he should win this easily. Getting good pictures?"

"Yes. Thank you so much for arranging this."

Ted smiled. He was a genuine, down-to-earth guy. "Glad I could help. He seems like a good man."

"He is."

The bell again sounded, beginning the final round and the last three minutes. There seemed to be a renewed energy, as if every second meant avoiding sudden death. Then the opponent landed a deadly combination, and Joe staggered back. Almost fell.

The crowd, sensing something, jumped to its feet. Ted placed his arm on Taylor's. "He'll be fine. He just lost some points, that's all. He's a beast."

Joe deflected the next set of blows and found his inner monster. The machine inside began a series of uppercut shots that had the challenger falling back. "See? He's back."

Sensing the advantage, Joe kept pummeling. The cheers around Taylor grew louder, and Joe never let up. She checked her immediate "Shouldn't he stop? The guy is about to go down." The level of intensity frightened her, yet at the same time called to something deep in her biology. Here was a defender, someone who protected those he loved and fought for justice and absolution.

After watching him fight, she'd never desired anyone

so much.

The bell rang, and within seconds the two men stood on either side of the referee, who took Joe's hand and thrust it high into the air. He'd won.

Joe stood there, as the crowd screamed and cheered for his win. Then as the ref let him go, he took off his headgear, and arm muscles bulged as he held his arms down out from his sides, gloves clenched palm side up, the muscles in his neck tightening and his eyes turning to slits as he opened his mouth to let out a primal scream, one Taylor captured. The emotions, so like Michael Phelps in 2008, went on for a few seconds before he pumped his fist into the air and seemed to float out of the ring.

As he disappeared from view, she headed back up the escalators to the suite. "Did you see that?" Marci asked when Taylor found her. "Your Joe was incredible."

"He's not my Joe."

"Well, then I want him to be my Joe, as did probably every woman in this place. He's smokin'."

"Hands off."

"Now the claws come out." Marci laughed. "Meow. You know you want him."

Taylor did. She sat in one of the comfortable chairs, scrolled through her images as Marci went off to the bar for another beer. The camera couldn't capture the true essence of the man, but it had come dangerously close. As Marci returned, Taylor tucked the camera away in her bag. She wasn't sure if tonight had made her a boxing fan, but it had shown Joe in another new light. She desired a man with too many dimensions to count.

Her phone beeped another text, from an unknown number. "Please stop blocking me. I just need to talk to you. It's urgent. Owen."

She deleted the text and blocked the new number, although really, she knew that wouldn't do anything. Owen could be extremely persistent.

"Oh Taylor, good, you're back," Virginia said. "I want to introduce you to a friend of mine. Ginger wants her family's portraits done, and I told her she must use you."

Taylor stood. "I'd be happy to help."

Virginia motioned. "Then follow me."

***

"Great job tonight, Joe," his trainer Hugh said as Joe exited the shower cubby clean and dressed in slacks and a red mesh polo. "The streak continues."

Joe rolled his shoulder. Tomorrow he'd have a few bruises, but nothing he couldn't handle. "He almost got me. That's never happened."

"I'll review the tape and figure out what went wrong."

"Thanks." Although Joe already knew the answer. The periphery of his vision had seen Taylor and her camera. One millisecond, but it had been enough. She'd been on the floor for his fight, and his body had forgotten the fight and instead wanted something else.

He'd paid for it by failing to block a fast combination to the head. Speaking of, he squinted his eyes a few times, trying to rid the headache that the two naproxen he'd ingested upon leaving the ring hadn't yet cured.

"See you in the gym Monday?" Hugh asked.

"Tuesday. I work tomorrow and Monday."

"Let's hope it's a light shift."

"That would be ideal." Joe rolled the other shoulder, stretching it out. "I'm not as young as I used to be."

His trainer gave him a pat on the back. "None of us are. See you. And again, great job."

"Thanks." Joe chatted with a few of his fellow competitors and then headed up to the suite.

Taylor was in conversation, but as soon as she saw him, she broke off and beelined over. "Congrats."

"Thanks."

He took a step toward the bar, but Taylor pressed a hand on his arm. He stopped. Gazed at her. "Can we get out of here?" she asked.

"Sure." He didn't need to socialize. Usually after a fight he'd head home, maybe grab some food. "We can go whenever, wherever you'd like."

Taylor glanced over her shoulder. Joe saw the woman who'd been at the photo shoot in conversation with some guy. "Damn. I drove Marci and—"

Joe nodded. "It's okay. No worries." Her hand never left his arm.

"Give me a minute."

As she moved away, he retrieved a soda from the bar and watched her speak with her friend. Then she was back, purse in hand. "Marci says Thad will give her a ride home."

"Thad?"

Taylor led the way out of the suite. "He's the son of someone here. In medical school at Wash U. I try not to judge. She's a big girl. So you don't want to stay around?"

Joe shook his head as they made their way down the escalators to the exit. "No. I normally go home, get some food Sometimes go to my parents. Man you. . ."

They'd reached the ground level. She turned to him. "What? I didn't catch that last part."

Only a few people lingered in the area by the box office, most inside cheering the current bout. He pulled her to him, inhaling the floral of her shampoo. "I said you smell so good."

Her hands were flat on his chest.

"Come home with me."

"Joe, I . . ."

He could see in her eyes she wanted the same thing. "You drive me crazy. To distraction." Admitting the truth didn't lift a burden.

"I did get you hit." She reached up to touch his chin and he winced. "Sorry."

"Lost concentration for a split second, yes," he admitted. "My own damn fault."

"Still." Her hands kept checking his injuries.

Joe looked at her and knew he was lost. She was touching him and driving him crazy. He couldn't go multiple rounds with her. Couldn't put her safely in a box. "I can't fight this—us—anymore."

"Then take me home," she whispered, and Joe couldn't

say no. Didn't want to.

Because she was in flats, he leaned down to kiss her. His mouth wasn't gentle as he found hers, for his need had consumed him. He kissed past her lips, thrusting his tongue so he could taste her mouth, so he could fully possess her. He deepened the kiss until she made that soft little kittenish cry. He pulled back, stared into her eyes. He was hard as a rock.

"Yes," she breathed. "My mom came home today so I don't have to take care of the cats."

He grabbed her hand. Led her out to the parking lot. "Where are you?"

"Over there. You?" Her chest heaved, and as they reached the car Joe pressed her up against her car door and kissed her senseless again. His hand found her breast, kneaded through the fabric. He'd take her right here but she deserved much more, and he wanted to take his time. Wanted to lose control for once. Wanted to trust that this time would be different. That she was different.

"Wait here until I bring my truck around. You can follow me. I live in St. Louis Hills. It's not far."

She appeared dazed as he helped her into her car. Good. He wanted her as affected as he was. "Hold that thought and I'll see you in a few."

The kiss stayed with Taylor the fifteen minutes it took her to drive to a four-family apartment building on the South Side. She parked behind the building, next to his pickup.

Few lights were on, which meant Elaina was probably

out. Good, Joe thought as he led Taylor upstairs. He'd be off to work tomorrow before Elaina could question him about the strange car parked next to his.

Joe unlocked the door and tossed his keys into their spot on the small kitchen table. He closed the door, twirled Taylor, and pressed her up against it, his hands immediately finding her breasts, and his lips her mouth.

She moaned immediately. "Good," he mumbled, his fingers reaching for her hem so he could pull up her shirt and slide his hands over the bare skin of her stomach. "Oh God yes."

He slipped under the bra, pebbled her nipple. "So perfect."

"Last time we were in this position you made me . . ." she breathlessly told him, her words hardening him further.

"Well, you'll come a lot tonight," he promised.

"I thought you needed food."

"I do." He exposed her breasts and lowered his mouth to a peak, licked his tongue over it. "But real food can wait. I want to taste you."

As he drew her nipple into her mouth, she trembled and went "oooh." He throbbed so hard it hurt more than the blows he'd taken tonight.

Brutus rubbed against his legs and then, not getting attention, bit him. "Hey."

Joe drew back, used his leg to push the cat aside. Taylor stood pressed up against his doorway, mouth swollen and clothing bunched. Her half-lidded eyes opened. "You have a cat."

"That monster right there. Brutus. Bad cat." Brutus simply licked an orange paw.

"He's sweet." She pulled her shirt down. "A good break. Let's get you some food."

"I liked what I was eating," he grumbled.

"It can wait until after you eat. Are you planning on stopping and running me off?"

He thought of his scarred skin. Manned up. "No. That was a mistake. Told you, I've been making a lot of them. But not tonight."

"Then let's eat. What do you have in this place?"

The kitchen was in the middle, with his bedroom behind. She pulled open the refrigerator door. "Is this roast beef good?"

"Yes. Bought it two days ago."

"Perfect." She grabbed that, some cheese, mayo, and the loaf of bread he also kept in the icebox. Then she made them both sandwiches.

"You know your way around a kitchen." His turn to open the refrigerator door, and he pulled out two bottles of beer. He held one up, and she took it.

"Thanks." She twisted the top off and took a swig. "I raid my mom's so much that I've become a professional forager. I couldn't believe she took extra days on me."

"But she's back now," Joe said, between big bites.

"Yes. I'd missed my apartment. It's not much, but it's mine. My first real space that's just mine, you know?"

"I've been here years. It's small, but all I really need."

"I noticed you had a very big TV."

He grinned. "A guy has to have some vices. I like movies. I don't even have cable, just Netflix. Really, that's all I need."

"So you're a simple man."

"Maybe?" He wasn't sure what she meant. She tore some of the roast beef from her sandwich and dropped it on the ground for the cat. "He's a monster."

Brutus put two paws on her leg and stood up on hind legs to ask for more. Taylor gave him another morsel before shooing him away. "He's a good boy. Like his owner."

"Honey, there's nothing good about me. Except maybe what I'm going to do to you in a few minutes. Although, actually, that's going to be great."

"Promises, promises." She winked at him, making him hard again. "We will see."

He swallowed the last bit of his food, so ready for her. He reached across the small table and toyed with the fingers on her free hand. "You should know something. About me." He hesitated. "For when we get naked. For we are getting naked." He emphasized the last word.

Taylor's plate was empty. "I already know."

He frowned, stunned. "Know what?"

She steadily held his gaze. "Why you wear those long socks that hide your legs."

He thumped against the chair back, breaking their connection. "Susie. She has a big mouth."

"She told me your own burns are why the book is so important to you, that's all. Now everything makes sense."

His need to make love to her warred with self-

169

preservation. "She shouldn't have said anything. It wasn't her place."

"Joe." Taylor leaned so she could grab his hand in hers. She squeezed. "You are more than your skin. I don't have sex with people based on how they look. It's the person inside. You matter. Hell, you'll only be the third person ever."

Warmth traveled from her touch. She didn't let him go, but rose to her feet and tugged him after her. He followed. "I'm glad she told me, because if you stop because you've got cold feet, I am going to be very unhappy. And you don't want me unhappy, do you? Not when you promised to make me happy?"

No, Joe didn't want that. He wanted her writhing under him as he plunged into her. He wanted her to be different, as he already believed her to be. "Let's make you happy."

"Let's." She led him into his bedroom, and before he could kiss her, she pushed him backward so his knees connected with the mattress and he sat on his bed.

He hadn't closed the blinds, so the room was awash with the glow from the streetlamps below. She leaned down to kiss him, and Joe shut his eyes and ceded control . . . for now. He let her kiss him, let her explore his mouth, and let her mate her tongue to his.

He moved his arm to reach for her, but she blocked his efforts and instead slid her lips down his neck. Her kisses on the sensitive skin of his neck created sweet torture. Then her hands grabbed for the polo waistband and up and off his shirt went, and he sat there with a bulge in his slacks and she stroked his entire hair-covered chest, and where her fingers weren't, her lips were.

Then her fingers found the belt buckle, and he resisted the urge to grab her hand and make her stop. He'd always been the one to direct foreplay, but he wanted this. Wanted to see what she'd do. His desire to trust conflicted with his controlling nature, so he let her have free reign. The rasp of the zipper going down had him sucking in a fast inhale, and her hand reaching into his boxers had him gasping for air. She was kryptonite. As she circled him and ran a thumb over his wet tip, resistance became futile. He'd let her do anything she wanted.

He kicked off his dress shoes, lifted his hips so she could remove his pants. She slid the garment to his knees, meaning most of his scars were still hidden. She cupped his sac and then she trailed tickling fingers down his inner thighs, down legs he widened to allow better access. She dropped to her knees before him, and he scooted to the edge of the mattress as she brought him into her mouth.

The air whooshed from his lungs as the wet heat of her mouth enveloped him. So sweet. His need balled into a fist as she circled him with her tongue as if he were a delicious sugar treat. He held back, wanting, craving to thrust. "Must stop . . ." he said, words jagged.

"No," she told him, her fingers making patterns on his inner thigh. Another hand cupped his balls, massaged, and his lower back arched as he couldn't resist any longer and spilled himself in shattering release.

Taylor's mouth kissed him through all of it, and he fell onto his back, spent. "Holy shit" was all he could say as his heart rate tried to recover from being shot to the stratosphere.

As he lay there, he'd never felt so vulnerable. He held himself still as she removed the rest of his clothes, exposing his skin. His breath hitched—waiting for the rejection or revulsion that didn't come. He made himself trust, began to relax as she touched her way down his calves, caressing the scars and the skin that lacked sensitivity. He pushed onto his elbows and then up to a seated position. Croaked out her name, "Taylor."

Her gaze locked onto his, held it without wavering as she rolled down the second sock and tossed it aside. Their eyes held as she kissed the inside of his calf, and Joe felt a tear threaten and bit his lip. Something inside him shifted. Cracked. She'd stripped him to his birthday suit, albeit now older and damaged, damage he knew she could see in the diluted light. She'd torn down every one of his walls. Before her, he was as open as day.

Normally he liked any sex pitch black, but that would mean he couldn't see Taylor, whose expression held something he'd never seen on any woman's face before. He fought back the worry and watched as she took a sip of the beer she'd brought in. "My turn," she said.

Then standing in front of him, she swayed her hips to silent music, crossed her arms in front of her and peeled off her shirt. He would never look at pink and black stripes the same way again. The push-up made globes of her breasts and its lacy edges hinted at her areolae. He began to move, but she shook her head, so he stayed put and enjoyed the shimmy as she stripped off the black jeans until she wore only the sexy bra and matching thong.

He hardened, not embarrassed to let her see how hot and ready he was again. She took a fingertip and drew a line down his shaft. With that, he moved. Took control back. He stood, drew her to him and crushed his mouth onto hers until he'd made her limp like a cooked noodle. He then threw back his comforter, flipped her into his arms, and placed her onto another one of his indulgences—six-hundred-count sheets as soft as butter.

Kissing her was heaven, and it was his turn to once again sample her body. This time instead of his fingers, he placed his mouth at her core and drank from her, indulging fully in the nectar he'd sampled from his finger after he'd left her house. He hadn't been able to help himself. Now he slid his palms under her and lifted her to his lips, drawing out wave after wave as she quaked and shattered. He drew back, placed two fingers against her slit to give her another shockwave. Her fingers had gripped the sheets, and he put the heel of one hand to her mound and then replaced his mouth with two fingers from his other hand, which he slid in and out until she came again.

Then he reached into the nightstand for a condom, from an unused box he'd had for what seemed like forever, and parting her legs, slid home.

As he entered her, Taylor's only cognizant thought was "Finally."

She wiggled to allow him deeper access, thrust her hands into that gorgeous, tempting hair. She clutched the strands, stroking both his head and his upper back as he went up on his elbows so he could push deep. His eyes had turned to a fathomless, deep blue gray, and she stared into them as she met him thrust for delicious thrust. His largeness stretched her, but her body accommodated and trembled as he rocked her world to another earthshaking orgasm, one whose heights were like nothing she'd experienced before. She clung to him, the intimate act sealing her fate. He'd claimed her, made her his.

Afterwards, they lay intertwined, and she could feel the scarred skin she'd touched earlier against her. She faced him and his hand found her breast and brought her nipple to a straining peak. He kissed her lips. "Good?" he asked between kisses.

"Great," she said. "You fulfilled your promise."

He slid a hand between her legs and circled, taking her wetness and making her even slicker. "Sweetheart, you haven't seen anything yet."

Chapter Ten

An exhausted Joe rolled into the firehouse at seven a.m. He'd had very little sleep.

Not that he minded. When he kissed her good-bye for the third time, this one out in the parking lot, he'd had no regrets. Neither had she.

They hadn't made any specific plans except to touch base sometime Tuesday about the next few photo shoots. As he worked the next weekend, he would be out of the loop.

"Lieutenant, congrats! We heard you won." Reid greeted as Joe entered the locker room. They all went on shift at the same time.

"I like how none of you losers bothered to show," Joe replied, hanging up his personal clothes. He was already in his blue pants and shirt. Given the hot June day, most of his guys were in regulation shorts.

"We'll be there at Guns 'N Hoses," Chris promised. "Have we missed that yet?"

"No," Joe conceded, shutting the locker.

Kyle tilted his head. "You look different."

"You would too if you went three rounds last night."

Kyle shook his head. "No, that's not it. You've got bags under your eyes."

"I do not."

"Yeah, you do. You either had a wicked case of insomnia or you got laid. Since that last one's not possible . . ." Kyle's eyes widened, and Joe knew he'd somehow given himself away. "You got laid."

"What?" Reid whipped around. "You got some?"

Chris peered closer. "Yeah, you can tell he did. Who was she?"

"It's the photographer. Has to be," Reid said. "I knew you liked her. Spill the details."

"As if," Joe retorted.

"We were getting worried about you. Did you give her the pink panties?"

"Hell no." Joe planted his hands on his hips, the memory of the little black and pink thong making his cheeks heat as part of him stirred. He better get them all moving before he embarrassed himself. "Don't you all have work to do?"

"We're still transitioning."

Joe knew that. While they technically weren't on the truck until eight a.m., the first hour was used for meetings, acclimation and checking equipment. Until eight, the previous crew was still on call.

"Was it good?"

The question of manhood demanded ne answer. "It was great. Now get the hell out of here."

"Our lieutenant's in love." Reid gave a whistle. "Hell is freezing over."

"Ha-ha. Keep it up and you'll be on bathroom duty for a month," Joe threatened.

"Enjoy it while you can. You marry them, and it tapers off when the kids come," Chris said. "Not that that's going to happen to me."

"The man's engaged and thinks he's a relationship expert," Reid quipped.

"And no one said anything about marriage," Joe added.

"But you know she's thinking it," Reid said. "All women do. Except maybe your sister Elaina."

"You better not be having sex with my sister."

Reid backpedaled. "No. No. Of course not."

Uncertain, Joe rolled his eyes and strode toward the office that would be his for the next two days. He pulled out his cell and checked. Nothing. He'd told her to text him if she needed anything. Of course that had been hardly an hour ago. So why was he checking like some giddy high school boy?

"Joe."

He paused. His captain was in the stationhouse and stood there with Lieutenant Mike Dexter, whose shift Joe was about to replace. "Hey chief. Dex. What's up?"

"Just wanted to say good job last night," the chief said. "Thought he might have had you for a minute there, but you pulled it out."

"Had it all the time," Joe said.

"Glad to hear it. We're counting on you in November. Want to keep the title. Feel free to rest up today if you're not busy. You look like it was a long night."

"Thanks." It had been a long and delicious night, one Joe couldn't wait to repeat.

***

Taylor's meeting with her applied project chair started at two, and amazingly she was running on time. She'd left Joe's around six a.m., gone home and straight back to bed, this time for much needed sleep, sleep she'd gotten in short snatches before Joe had woken her up and taken her all over again before he'd had to leave for work.

Her body felt delightful sore in all the right places, and she had that eternal optimism that comes after being warm and cherished and held tenderly.

She kept that optimistic buzz until the end of her presentation, when her professor told her, "I'm just not feeling this. What you've proposed doesn't push the envelope. Yes, it's a photo story like you'd see in *New York Times*. But your goal was to make more of a personal connection. I'm not feeling that level of deep emotion."

She stood in front of the projector screen, the large image of Susie behind her. "But that's what this book is about."

He shook his head, took off his wire rim glasses, and

wiped off some lint. "No, it's about healing. It's about humanity. While these are multiple subjects celebrating their lives, I'm thinking that it might be better for you to focus on one person and show a character arc. Connect us to this little girl, for instance. Go behind her daily life."

"She's in Maine for the rest of the summer."

He shrugged. "Then pick someone else. For instance, who is the one behind the book? Whose idea was it?"

"Joe. He's a firefighter. He's Susie's brother."

"I take it he's burned?"

She sucked in a breath. "How did you know?"

"Educated guess. As a media communications professional, we study people. That's part of our job, as we are reporting on their lives. We choose what to reveal and what to hide. Show me pictures of Joe. Surely you have some."

"Yes, but not of his burns. I haven't gotten to him yet."

"Why not?" Her professor drummed his fingers nonstop, that annoying habit she hated but had to tolerate. She reminded herself that her professor had come in on a Sunday since she had work all the rest of the week and since he'd been out of town. "Surely you have others of him."

"I do, but—"

"Show me." His tone brooked no argument.

So Taylor clicked on a folder and brought up the family shots. Her professor said nothing as she ran through them and, worried about his silence, she opened another folder and showed him the untouched photos of Joe boxing. "I took these last night, so I haven't done anything to them yet."

The photos were in the order she'd taken them, so there was Joe in quiet contemplation in the locker room lacing and unlacing. Then she had him in the ring, right down to the primal victory scream.

"This man is your subject."

"My subject."

"Yes, him and no one else. You've captured who he is, but you've only begun to scratch the surface. How was he burned?"

"Grass fire when he was twelve."

"And his sister was in the middle of it?"

Her professor was perceptive. "Yes. He went in to save her."

"How did the fire start?"

"I don't know."

Her professor tapped a pen against the wood conference table. "Find out. There's a story there or he wouldn't be doing all this."

"He couldn't save her in time and she was injured. It's why he's a firefighter today."

Her professor rose to his feet so he stood even with her. "Taylor, this is your subject. A series of ten to twenty portraits that reveal the inner workings of this man. He's clearly a family guy, but he also has a Neanderthal need to climb into the ring and pummel some other guy senseless. This is your project, and it's one I can easily approve, which would allow you to get your diploma—should you deliver it to me within the next three weeks before summer session ends. You do want to graduate, don't you?"

"Yes."

"Then get him to let you photograph his burns. You'll need that one special cornerstone shot that lets me see inside his soul. The rest are up to you, so long as you reveal who he is." He pointed to the shot of Joe screaming with victory. "That's a great picture. I'll look forward to seeing the rest. E-mail me when you're ready. And, no promises, but be good enough and you might still make the juried exhibition."

With that, he left. Taylor fell into one of the leather conference chairs with a hard thump. She leaned back, swiveled, and stared up at Joe's picture. All her previous bouncy energy evaporated. Take Joe's photos.

The man couldn't even go into the boxing ring without being covered up. He'd left her mother's house that first day rather than reveal he'd been burned, something she'd have discovered the moment he dropped his pants. Joe Marino was a complicated individual. She might have broken down a huge barrier last night, but she knew she still had far more walls to tear down, and if she told him about this, he'd reinforce all the ones still standing. Susie wanted him in the book, but even she'd abdicated the problem of Joe's agreement to Taylor.

"Private" described Joe perfectly. She remembered his words "No choice," words she'd mocked. She realized he wouldn't be Mr. September if some higher up hadn't chosen him and given him an ultimatum.

He hid vulnerability beneath that tough guy exterior

and cheeky, charming attitude.

She closed the screen on her laptop so the excited figure on the screen vanished into black. She had to graduate. There was no way she could afford another semester. She had no other options.

Joe Marino was now her applied project.

Chapter Eleven

"So you made Joe your project?" Marci blinked in disbelief as Taylor carried over two glasses of water. "Are you crazy?"

"I don't have a choice," Taylor protested, passing over a glass. Neither had wanted alcohol tonight. Taylor sighed. She hadn't planned on telling Marci about Joe, but shortly after Marci's arrival, the secret had slipped out. Marci was her best friend. Had been there through thick and thin. She knew she could trust her with the moral quandary Taylor now found herself in.

Marci, not even in the apartment a full ten minutes before Taylor had blurted out the truth, made herself comfortable by kicking her feet up onto Taylor's coffee table. The AC wasn't doing a good job, and Taylor made a mental note to call the landlord. The window unit probably needed to be replaced, or at least recharged.

"You know he's not going to go for it. What am I going to do? I have to graduate." Taylor paced. "I haven't even asked him to pose for me. He's not going to agree."

After her meeting with her professor, she'd been processing images of Joe all day until Marci had popped by and distracted her. They'd even ordered pizza, which was on the way. "Joe likes to help people. Surely he'll do this one thing for me." Taylor spoke aloud, as if that would help make Joe agree.

"True." Marci nodded. Drank more water. Talked while Taylor paced. "Thanks for asking me to go last night. It was a good match. I don't think I've ever had that much fun. Thad and I went out dancing afterwards."

"Clearly he got you home safe and sound," Taylor replied, grateful Marci had temporarily distracted her from her dilemma.

Marci drained the glass, leaned back. "I don't know how safe it was, but he was sound all right."

"Marci. You didn't."

Marci shook her head. Fanned herself. "No, we just had a great make out session in his car and I sent him on his way. The sun was coming up. I'd prefer my neighbors not see me in a car that early in the morning. God knows what they already think of me."

Taylor arched her eyebrows.

"Seriously," Marci returned with an exasperated sigh. "No shaking of the peaches or playing with the sausage because I'm trying to turn over a new leaf. But believe me, I wanted to. It was hard to say no to asking him up, or to say no to having sex in a Porsche, but I did . . . say no, that is. A damn convertible Porsche. Anyway, he says he'll call, but they all say that. I doubt he'll even text."

Taylor tried to encourage her friend. "Perhaps this time will be different."

"Not holding my breath. Have you ever felt the leather of a Porsche?" Marci sighed. "It's heaven. So soft. Smooth. Like, I've never felt anything like it. He's going to want to date someone from his social class. I don't stand a chance. I was a hook-up he didn't get."

"You don't know that."

"Well, I'm not holding my breath, you know? I've done that far too many times to waste any more energy. Mr. Right is out there, but why is he so damn much work to find?"

"You're preaching to the choir," Taylor admitted.

"I know. I know. So how was the rest of your night with Joe?"

Taylor leaned back in the low armchair and said nothing. Marci's eyes widened. "Do you mean to tell me you and he . . ."

Taylor nodded. Blushed. Her skin heated. She waved a hand in her face to create a breeze.

"Oh, I want details." Marci leaned forward. "Spill."

"His place. It was good."

"Just good?"

Taylor blushed again.

"Yeah, I thought so." Marci smirked. "A man like that has got to be damn good. So who seduced who?"

"Mutual, but I took charge. It was different somehow. There's a connection there. Something I'd never felt before."

"Like in your books?"

"Better." Taylor hadn't read any more about Duncan since Joe had first kissed her. "I've never been so turned on."

Marci began to chew on an ice cube, the motion making loud crunching sounds. "Well, wow. I thought you said he didn't want you."

"Things changed."

Marci chomped more ice. Rattled her glass. "Amazing. Have you heard from him?"

Taylor automatically gazed at her phone, which sat silent on the counter. "He's at work the next two days. He sent me a brief text telling me he was at the firehouse and making sure I'd gotten home safe. I said yes, and that's been it."

"He's probably really busy."

"I assume so. I have no idea what firefighters do except for what I've seen on TV."

Taylor's phone beeped with a message. "Maybe that's him now."

Taylor retrieved Marci's empty water glass. Refilled it. Grabbed her phone on the way back. "No, it's some strange number."

She unlocked her phone, opened the text. Marci craned her neck. "Is it Joe?"

Taylor's skin chilled as she read it, as if the temperature in the apartment had dropped twenty degrees. "No. Owen. This is the third number he's used. Why doesn't he get that I don't want to talk to him."

"Let me read it."

Marci stretched out her hand, but Taylor didn't release the phone. Instead she read it aloud. "It says, 'Taylor, I promise this isn't like last time. I only need a few minutes of your time. Please speak to me. I can meet you at Presley's if that makes you feel safer. Please answer me. It's urgent. Owen.'"

"That's crazy."

"He's crazy." Taylor shivered. Drew a green fuzzy blanket over her, despite the pathetic AC.

"Answer him. Tell him to go to hell. In fact, hand me the phone and I'll do it." Marci thrust her palm forward.

"No. I can't. I don't want to have to change my phone number again. I lost clients last time. Most photographers have a contact number online, but I can't even put up a website. I'm hoping that if I don't respond, he's going to think he has the wrong number and stop texting me. He's got to think he's dialing the wrong person."

"So send one back saying you're not Taylor."

"He's too smart. He'll see through that. He's pretty sharp. Someone gave him this number, so he knows it's mine. I have to keep ignoring him."

Marci frowned. "You should contact the police."

"For what? Text messages? I got a restraining order last time and *that* didn't help. Besides, the police have better things to do."

"Taylor, you have to take care of yourself. Abuse is serious."

"I know that and I will. I've been extra vigilant. I don't

understand why now, after all this time."

"Maybe you should tell Joe."

Taylor crossed her arms. Drew her blanket higher. "Why would I tell Joe?"

"He's probably got friends on the police force. Maybe he can have one of them do some sniffing around, off-book. You know, see what's really going on. Spy on Owen."

Taylor loved Marci, but she was so naïve. "This isn't a TV show."

"Well, I don't know. It was just a suggestion. I'm worried about you." Marci appeared more upset than Taylor felt.

"I told you he was with a girl at Presley's, so I don't know why he'd start contacting me again. It makes no sense. But eventually he'll go away. He'll stop."

"So maybe take Joe and go meet up with Owen. You said Joe likes to help. And you slept with him, so he's sort of your guy now, right? Have him scare off your ex. I'm sure he'll do it if you ask."

"Great. So I have to ask him about taking his burn pictures and about scaring off my ex? This is getting worse and worse. I'll handle Owen myself."

"If you say so." Marci puckered her lips. "I wouldn't. Make Joe feel needed."

Taylor voiced the truth. "One time in bed doesn't constitute a relationship. Hell, I don't even know what we are. We had chemistry. The next time I see him, he may have me all out of his system. We do have to work together to finish the book."

"I think you're making a mistake. My two cents." Marci's feet thumped to the floor as she sat up. She leaned over and touched Taylor's arm. "I'm worried about you. You turned into a basket case last time. I know. I was there."

Taylor jutted her chin. Remained stubborn. "And I'm glad you were, but that won't happen this time. It's been two years. I'm not feeling guilty anymore, as if his behavior was somehow my fault." She swiped and deleted the text message without answering it. "I have too much on my plate to let Owen be a distraction."

"I don't want you turning some corner and then he shoots you."

"This is real life not TV." Although Taylor would never admit that was one of her worst fears, even though in all of the craziness that had gone down, she'd known Owen would never physically hurt her. He'd broken objects, shown up at her work and made a scene, and even towered over her and screamed in her face, but he'd never actually hit her. However, the rest had been terrifying and threatening enough. He'd been unstable, and she'd gotten help, protecting herself despite her fear. Having learned, she refused to be held hostage to fear ever again.

"I'll be fine. Despite his issues, I don't think Owen's going to be lurking around the corner with a gun."

"Taylor—" Marci began.

"Seriously." Taylor used the tone that indicated "drop it," which Marci thankfully did. "My bigger problem is getting Joe to agree to be photographed. How do I even bring that up without it seeming like I have that right since we had sex?"

"You could get him naked again and then ask."

Taylor sighed. "You are impossible."

"Which is why you love me," Marci teased. "Seriously, though, I'm not too good with my ideas today. Maybe it's the lack of sex. Maybe I should have jumped him. But I want to be respectable."

"You're trying, isn't that what counts?"

"I guess," Marci said.

"I'll talk to Susie. She got me into this. I should see her Wednesday for a shoot. I've actually got a busy week. I'm cramming in a family photo for Ginger Redmond. Did you meet her last night?"

Marci shook her head. "I got distracted. And there were a lot of people there."

"True." By the time Taylor and Joe had left, the suite had been at capacity because Virginia never did anything by half. "Well, her mother is in town this week from Arizona and she wants to get portraits done while everyone is together. So I worked her in."

"At least everything sounds like it's coming together photo-wise."

"Except for Joe. I can't just text him and ask, and I don't know when I'll see him next. We didn't make any plans."

"But you're working together."

"Yes, but still, no plans. It sounds like I'm in the when-will-he-call bind too."

The doorbell rang, and Taylor opened it and paid for the pizza delivery: Cecil Whittaker's green pepper and onion, dinner of the gods. "What are we watching tonight?" she asked, pointing to the DVD Marci had brought.

"The first *Thor* movie. I found myself needing some oldie but goodie movie man candy."

Taylor grinned. "That works. I can use a man candy break, especially if it involves Tom Hiddleston and Chris Hemsworth."

"Me too." Marci lifted her water glass in a toast and clinked it to Taylor's. "Me too."

Taylor picked up the DVD and put it in the machine. "Let's do this."

***

Tuesday morning at eight a.m., Joe walked out of the firehouse tired but strangely invigorated. While he'd been too busy to call Taylor, they'd exchanged a few texts. He'd agreed to attend the next photo session, today at five.

He'd planned on having Susie supervise this shoot, but given what had happened between him and Taylor over the weekend, he'd told his sister he'd be there. He'd let Susie read into it whatever she wanted. He didn't care. For once, he had hope. Joy. He hadn't seen revulsion in Taylor's eyes, but rather desire and lust and maybe a little glimmer of something else.

The photo shoot was at Forest Park, for Taylor

planned on putting the subject, a sixty-year-old architect, against the stone arches of the World's Fair Pavilion that had inspired his career. Word was his favorite movie was *Meet Me in St. Louis.*

Joe climbed into his pickup truck and checked the dashboard clock. He'd actually gotten off on time, giving him plenty of time to go home and get in a long run and a good hard climb before he had to meet both Taylor and Dalton Palenske. Joe sang off key all the way home, until his phone rang. He didn't recognize the caller, and let it go to voice mail. Upon exiting his truck, he retrieved the message.

"Joe? This is Marci. Taylor doesn't know I'm calling, because I swiped your number while she was in the bathroom the other night. It's urgent that I speak with you. She said you were off today. This is my cell. I'm working until two, but you can reach me after that. Please don't tell her I called. I'll explain when we talk."

What the heck?

For a nanosecond Joe stared at his phone, as if somehow the answer would magically appear. He replayed the call, listening to the nuances of Marci's voice. He went through the message one more time, hearing guilt mixed with worry mixed with a need to not be discovered. Mostly, though, he heard worry, and Joe didn't like that one bit.

He went inside, deliberately stopping his mind from racing through all the various scenarios that threatened, scenarios that ranged from everything like Taylor was hiding a contagious or communicable disease to that she was already married or had committed some crime. The last two were silly, which is why he fed the cat, grabbed a G2, and headed to the gym. His problem-solving brain needed to be diverted, and there was nothing like hanging forty-two feet in the air to clear one's brain.

But by two p.m., even after getting in a ten-mile run, he hadn't achieved a true sense of calm. He'd been able to escape his racing thoughts, but he hadn't been able to push them far enough away. They'd lurked like a shadow: *What did Marci need to tell him?*

His early morning glow had long faded, replaced by agitation. Maybe it wasn't about Taylor at all. But Joe's gut said otherwise for, if it wasn't about her, why would it have to be secret? Maybe it was happier news, like perhaps Marci was throwing Taylor a birthday party. Joe frowned. He had no idea when her birthday was. Why did those things always seem so irrelevant? Or Facebook dependent, something Taylor wasn't even on.

Once home, he dialed Marci a minute after two. His fingers tightened as the phone kept ringing. He was going to get her voice mail, but at the last second she answered. "Hello?"

"It's Joe Marino."

He heard the relief in her voice. "Joe. Thank God."

Years of training kept his adrenaline in check and his voice casual. He knew instinctively this was not going to be about a happy birthday party. "What's up?"

"It's Taylor. She's . . ." She hesitated. He waited. She'd speak when ready, and his job had taught him to keep silent until that occurred. "Has Taylor ever mentioned Owen?"

"The ex? The one there the night of the Pink Out charity server event?"

"So you saw him?" Marci's voice rose a notch, and more agitation powered through Joe.

He somehow remained calm. "Yeah. Table of four. Two guys and two girls. He seemed pretty tight with one of the girls. Marci, what's going on?"

"Well, she and Owen ended badly."

"She told me that. Said she was shocked seeing him."

"That's an understatement. When it ended, she had to get a restraining order against him. It expired a year ago."

Joe was flabbergasted. No wonder Taylor had hidden from Owen that night, ditched the table. He wished she'd told him. How could he help if he didn't know the full story?

He checked his anger. "She didn't tell me that part."

"That's Taylor. She hates asking for help. The breakup was two years ago, and she thought she'd never see him again. She changed apartments. Changed phone numbers. She's not even on any social media and doesn't have a web site. But he's contacting her again. She's ignoring it. She can't believe he'd hurt her. We had to push her to get the order, she's so damn stubborn."

That Joe knew firsthand. Marci continued. "He stalked her. He was crazy obsessive." She paused, and he could imagine her chewing her lip. "She'll kill me if she knew I'm telling you this, but I'm worried about her. I was there earlier today when he sent her a text message asking her to get in touch, telling her it's urgent."

A wave of pure protectiveness roared over Joe. He took a deep breath, worked to stay in control so his words didn't sound angry. "She didn't tell me."

"You can't let her know I told you. She wants to handle it on her own, but he's texted her at least once since Sunday when I saw her, and whatever she says, I don't think he's going to leave her alone."

He loosened his grip, his hand a solid vise. "I'm glad you told me."

"I probably shouldn't have. You two are . . . well, I don't know exactly what you are, but I hoped perhaps you had a friend who's a cop and can warn him off or something? I don't want to see her hurt again."

"You did the right thing. She shouldn't handle this by herself." He omitted the part of how Taylor was being a stubborn fool, for that's what she was.

"You'll take care of it?" Marci sounded hopeful.

"I'm trained to help. It's what I do. And, if nothing else, Taylor is my friend, and I take care of my friends."

"Thanks."

Joe hung up. Now, Taylor's reaction that night made sense. Brutus wove between his legs. He had less than three hours before he saw her again, time enough to work out how to bring up the sensitive subject. He wanted her to tell him. For her to ask for his help. He didn't want to go behind her back, didn't want secrets between them. However, he would do just that if necessary.

***

Dalton Palenske was a character. A real hoot, actually, Taylor thought as she finished his pictures. As an architect specializing in preserving historic buildings,

he'd worn a blue and white pinstripe seersucker suit and a white bowler hat reminiscent of something from the 1904 St. Louis World's Fair.

That was if people dressed that way during the fair. Taylor wasn't a historical fashion expert. But by the end of the shoot, she definitely was a Dalton fan. He'd cracked bad jokes nonstop, stretching the marbled skin on his burned face into a wide smile. He waved his white cane, the one with the brass knob on top. "Can't wait to see these. Missus always said I'd need a good picture for the obit."

"That's cold," Joe returned with a chuckle.

"You don't know my wife," Dalton parried, that warped grin stretching further. Taylor could tell he was joking, that he really loved his wife. "Marielle will talk your ear off." He touched his left ear. "Good thing I'm hard of hearing."

"Well, you have plenty of good years left," Taylor said as she handed Joe the camera. "I have a way of knowing these things. Not to worry, you'll be listening to Marielle for eons to come."

He waved his left forefinger, the one that was missing a tip after having been removed post-burn. "Lucky for you she had garden club today, or she'd be telling you how to do your job."

"Speaking of my job, mind if I let Joe try a few? He's learning."

"Trying to teach an old dog new tricks? With this guy? Don't hold your breath." Dalton laughed. "Get it? He's a firefighter. Smoke? Holding your breath? . . . Ah, tough crowd."

Dalton didn't seem too upset about his flat joke; he shifted his weight, his white patent wingtips shined to a high gloss. "You ever gonna be ready, Joe?"

"You don't want to look bad, do you?"

"Crossed that bridge years ago. No photo you take can hurt me now." He patted the stone archway. "Love this place. She's been a good shoulder all these years. Used to come and sit here, look out over the grass and the fountain, and remember that I was alive and that was all that mattered. Thanks for letting me do these here."

Taylor watched the hand that had seen many reconstructive surgeries lovingly caress the stone. "No problem," she told Dalton. "Making you happy is what makes me happy."

While the original intent had been a series of studio portraits, she'd quickly realized that each of the survivors had a unique story, and allowing them input into their backgrounds had calmed nerves and made for a better overall experience.

"No, try holding the camera vertically." She touched Joe's hand, and he turned it as she indicated. She stepped back, giving him space. One brief touch put her body on a sexual high alert. After a marathon bout of lovemaking a few days ago, her body had missed his. Craved his touch. Being near him stirred all sorts of feelings. Desires.

"Okay Dalton, tilt your chin to the right. A little more. There. Perfect." The shutter whirred as Joe took the shots.

He'd become better with the camera, she noted; he'd become more confident. "You look fabulous."

"Of course I do," Dalton returned, with a smile Joe captured before he lowered the camera.

"We're good."

"No, I'm great," Dalton returned with a laugh. "I'm your best subject."

"You're my only subject."

"See?" He strolled over, as if without a care in the world. "By the way, we're getting a major motion picture coming through that will be looking for runners to be part of a marathon race. You interested? I've got some pull with the casting." He winked at Taylor. "My wife."

Joe shrugged. "If my schedule allows."

"Won't pay much, but as soon as Marielle begins casting for extras, I'll shoot you an e-mail. Could be fun if you can do it. I'll be in touch with you, too, missy. Can't wait to see my shots."

"You mean I don't get to be in a movie?" she teased.

He winked. "Okay. Twist my arm. I'll see what I can do, but it's up to the missus."

"I'll have your proofs in about six or seven days,"

Taylor told him.

"Call my wife and she'll set something up. She knows where I am more than I do."

Taylor laughed, shook his hand. "Will do."

"Good to see you," Joe said, taking Dalton's outstretched hand.

Dalton reached around and clasped Joe's hand in both of his. "Thanks for doing this, son. Talk soon."

With that he strolled off toward his BMW, swinging his cane the entire way.

"He's a funny guy," Taylor observed.

"Don't let the deadpan fool you. He's sharp as a tack, and his wife is a saint. He's responsible for a lot of the North and South Side's recent redevelopment projects. He has a heart of gold. A real man of the people. Worked his way up from nothing."

"He told me his burns were from a fire."

"House fire when he was ten. Started when a kerosene heater malfunctioned. He saved his younger brother. He'll tell you his burns were a small price to pay."

She'd found the opening she'd needed. "What about you?"

"Me what?" He frowned.

"Well, you saved Susie." She put her camera in the bag. She hesitated. Blurted it all out in a rush. "Look, I don't know how to say this, but I think you should be in the book."

"No." His answer came swift and fast.

"You need to tell your story." Taylor swung her camera

bag onto her shoulder.

"No." He strode off, held out his hand, and indicated she should take it. She caught up, and he guided her down the walkway toward the fountain.

"Are you going to give me a reason?" Taylor asked, his hand firm in hers.

"I'm already in a stupid calendar with my shirt off. That's enough. This project was never to be about me. So no."

He could be stubborn, too, couldn't he? She sighed as they stopped at the fountain's edge. Behind them the century-old pavilion rose from the ground, majestic red roof seeming to kiss the sky. "I can see why Dalton likes it here."

"Quieter than Art Hill. Not as many people."

"Unless there's a wedding. I photographed one here once. Wedding and reception both under the pavilion and on the terrace. It was lovely."

"Sounds like it," Joe said, kicking a small pebble. A silence fell between them, the only sound the water cascading down into the reflecting pool below. On occasion a car honked down on Government Drive as the driver wove around the cyclists.

She sighed. "Please do the photo."

"No." He stared at water that shot into the air before cascading down a series of terraces.

"I know you mean well, but understand that I can't."

"Why? Help me understand."

He went to the water's edge. Sat on the concrete ledge.

"I'm not the one worthy of sympathy. I'm the whole reason Susie was burned. It's my fault."

Confusion had her brow knitting. "That makes no sense. You tried to save her. How is it your fault?"

A dark shadow crossed his face despite the full sun. "Believe me, I wish it weren't true." He inhaled deeply and exhaled a harsh breath that sent one of his long, dark strands heavenward. He raked a hand through his hair, jerking the wayward lock back into place.

"Joe?"

His beautiful eyes had turned angry, bitter. "How is it possible? Believe me, I ask myself that every day."

He was mad at himself. She reached forward to touch his hand, but he pulled away. "I don't understand."

He gave a harsh, bitter laugh. "It's quite simple. I never should have had to have saved my sister."

"But you did. You were a hero."

"No." He shook his head, violently sending those locks swinging again. "No, never say that. I'm no hero. I wanted to watch something burn. Fire fascinated me. I wanted to control it, like my dad. Instead, I'm the stupid kid who scarred my sister for life with a fire I never should have started. And there's no way I can ever forgive myself for that."

***

As the confession left him, Joe wanted to take it back. Retract his words. For he saw Taylor's eyes widen. He saw the horror. The disgust. The shock. Oh, she masked her reaction quickly, but he saw it, as he'd known he would.

"Joe . . ."

He slid about a foot away. "No, don't pity me. I've had enough of that to last a lifetime."

Hurt had her lower lip quivering, and his finger itched to touch it. "Whatever you do, don't you dare say you're sorry."

She folded her hands in her lap. Stared at him, not knowing what to say.

So he filled in for her. "Do you see why I can't do the book?"

Below they could hear two kids calling out to each other. "Maybe that's the whole reason you should do the book. Maybe it's time to let that battle go," she suggested.

"Like you have with Owen?"

Her mouth formed a horrified O, and Joe hated himself. Damn. When he'd first met her, she'd called him a cad. She'd been one hundred percent right, especially after he'd hit her with that low blow. "Owen means nothing to me," she insisted.

"No, but he's stalking you again and you refuse to do anything about it."

"Marci." She fumed. Scowled. Glared at him. "You talked to Marci."

He didn't confirm or deny. "You want me to pose for the book. Do you know what you're asking?"

She nodded. "Yes. You'd have to expose yourself."

"Which I don't want to do. Tell me, why should I

show my scars to the world? Why should I do this when you won't tell him to take a hike, or even ask for help?"

"I will handle Owen on my own."

"And until you let me help you deal with Owen, I'm not going to be in the book. We each want something. Quid pro quo. You'll have to meet me halfway."

Her frustration grew. "You are impossible."

"Pretty much." Oddly, he'd calmed. Lost the anger that occurred every time he thought of what he'd done. "You know, I thought I could handle things. I was twelve. I'd used matches before. I was a Boy Scout. I'd show Susie how to start a fire. How to put one out. To this day, it's a blur how things got out of control, how we were suddenly in the middle of a burning field with no way out. So while you may think you can handle things, while you may think it's all fine, trust me, in the next second it can all go straight to hell."

"He threatened. But he never—"

Joe cut her off. "Even verbal abuse is too much. I've been on too many calls. Seen too many things."

Silence stretched. Finally she admitted, "I don't know what to say or do. He is scaring me."

"Say you'll let me help. Don't be one of those calls."

"I won't be. And no. This is my problem."

"Let me help," he insisted.

"Let me take your picture." She sighed, watched a pair of sparrows as they circled and made figure eights. Joe reached out and touched her hand. Took it into his, where it warmed, felt right. He knew what he had to do.

"I'm a big believer in compromise. You let me help with Owen and I'll let you take my picture."

"For the book."

He didn't pull away, a first. "It's a big step for me to even let anyone see my skin, much less let it be made into a permanent record. Can we start with the photo shoot, go from there?"

She nodded. "Yes."

"So you agree? My picture and you let me help with Owen."

"Yes," she repeated.

He felt the tension drain away. "Good. We'll cross all the other bridges as we come to them. Deal with things together. Sound good? And I'm sorry if I've been an ass."

"You're a sensitive guy in a tough guy exterior. I get it."

He still had hold of her hand. Brought it to his chest as if branding him.

"Well, you've broken through. Made me mush. Made me want to kiss you as if it were as essential as breathing."

He felt her fingers tremble. "Then why aren't you?"

"Because we're in a very public park and I wouldn't stop, and what I want to do to you would get us arrested." He took her hand, moved the fingertips to his lips and kissed each one.

"Maybe we should leave. My place is five minutes away. The AC is still on the fritz, but—"

His mouth found hers, tasted the sweetness that was fast becoming the nectar he needed for life. "Let's go."

***

He was the first man she'd brought home to her new apartment. As she opened the door, she felt shy. Nothing was fancy. His TV could swallow hers twice. Her furniture was mismatched hand-me-downs, the plaid couch arriving after her mother's latest redecorating binge and the chair a garage sale gift from her sister. At least she'd straightened up this morning—no hand-washed undies draped over the white ladder-back kitchen chairs.

She gestured. "This is it. Can I get you anything?"

"Absolutely." He tugged her against him and wrapped his arms around her waist. "There's definitely something I want." His mouth came down on hers, nipped lightly. "Some of this." He teased her lips, brought his hand up to cup her breast. "And definitely some of this."

Her knees liquefied. Heat pooled. He intensified the kiss, feathered his fingertips over her chin, and lightly drew a line down her neck to the hollow of her throat. Her eyelids fluttered closed and she snuggled closer, wanting to close any gap.

Touching him created anticipation, yet it was also like coming home. She could lose herself and be totally safe. She molded her mouth to his, the tingles traveling to her toes expanding tenfold. She grabbed his hand, wanting to be even closer. "Follow me."

She led him into her bedroom. Here she'd splurged, buying a brass bed she'd found on Craigslist. She'd found a bright floral comforter set, the edge of which he was already drawing back. She fell with him onto the bed, the mattress giving and their clothes flying as they came together skin to skin.

She liked the weight of him, the way his body joined with hers. She cried as he filled her, as he shattered her body into a million delicious pieces, every nerve heightened with pure bliss.

Joe was a slice of heaven on earth, and she clutched him close as her body, slick with sweat, began to come down, the trembles ebbing.

He reached over, wiped her brow. "Good."

She could only nod. Blink a time or two, for he'd brought her almost to tears, their lovemaking had been that special.

"I'm glad." His legs wove between hers, and she barely noticed the roughened texture. "I hate fighting. This is so much better."

She nodded. Her head drooped. "Agreed," she mumbled sleepily. He'd worn her out. "We can plan later."

"We will," he promised, and with that, she curled up in his arms, secure that all would be well.

Chapter Twelve

The next two days passed uneventfully. Almost settled into a routine. Off Tuesday through Friday, Joe would meet Taylor later in the evening after her photo shoots. He maintained his hours of daily training—he planned on running the St. Louis Rock 'N' Roll marathon in October and wanted to either win his age group or place in the top five.

They'd go out to eat, or go to the movies, and then spend hours at one or the other's apartment. He'd agreed to let her photograph him, but hadn't yet determined where, which is why Friday morning found him out driving around trying to decide.

She'd suggested doing something associated with firefighting, but he'd nixed that idea, preferring something more along the line of simply wearing either his boxing shorts, his workout gear, or his racing wear. An industrial setting perhaps. Or against the shimmery steel of the Gateway Arch, which during the summer months heated up until almost unbearable to touch. Or maybe the graffiti wall of the downtown Riverfront Trail, which he was about to go run. He parked his truck. Stepped out into the heat. Hit the remote.

His phone buzzed, and he reached into his pocket. He recognized the number. "Hey Harry."

"Hey. Got your message. Sorry I didn't get back to you until now. Had a big case I was working on. What's up?"

"Need a favor." He'd known Detective Harry Wright since high school, trained with him many times. So Joe explained Taylor's situation with Owen. "She's a friend and I care about her, but she refuses to do anything. Can you help?"

"Yeah, let me do some digging. Find out what's going on, see if there's anything we can do. Give me a few days. I'll be in touch."

"That'll work. I'm grateful for any help."

"You can buy the next round."

"That'll work too." Joe put his phone away, checked his shoelaces, and began his run.

***

In the end, he decided to do his pictures in a field. It was Susie's idea, and that Sunday, the last day of June, after he'd worked the weekend shift, he and Taylor drove out to rural St. Charles, to a farm a friend owned. She climbed out of the truck, grabbed her camera, and shut the door. "This place is perfect."

She glanced around at the quintessential farm, complete with red barn with white trim and those blue metal siloes. A few chickens pecked at the ground. Black angus grazed in one pasture and in another, corn reached knee high. A tabby cat slept on the wraparound porch of a low-slung ranch house. "Are they here?" she asked.

"No. We have the place to ourselves for a few hours." He strode toward a metal gate, undid the chain, and slipped into the pasture. She followed. "Watch where you step."

"Will do," Taylor said, making sure she didn't place her Converse in what Missourians referred to as a cow patty, otherwise known as a pile of cow poop. He waded out into the tall grass with the feathery tops.

He'd chosen to wear a pair of jean shorts and he stripped off his T-shirt, baring that chest she'd palmed with abandon. She licked her lips. "We forget to bring the Off," he called. "You'll have to check me for ticks later."

Sunlight brought out highlights in his dark hair that fell almost, but not quite, to his shoulders, and the wheat grass created shadows that danced over his skin. Her breath caught. He was the most attractive man, and her pictures would prove it. "I'm sure that won't be a problem as I'll need the same done for me. It's going to require getting naked you know."

He grinned wickedly. "That's the only part I'm looking forward to in all this. Let's get this done before I really start to itch. I'd prefer not to have to need dabs of pink calamine lotion."

She moved into a slightly flattened section of grass, lowered to her knees, and began to shoot. Like the first time they'd met, she issued instructions, telling him where to place his hands and how to stand. This time, though, she knew him and he relaxed, enjoyed himself. Less than fifteen minutes later, they were finished. "That's it. You're done," she called.

T-shirt in hand, he strode over. "Let me see."

"How about we get that shower first?" She slapped at her leg. "Now I'm itching. We can take one together."

"Yeah, a shower would be good." He kissed her lightly on the lips. "I'm ready for the naked part."

He certainly was, Joe realized, his fingers tightening on the wheel during the drive. She'd seen his scars. Touched them. He'd shared his deepest secret with her—that he'd caused the fire—and she was still around. That thought amazed him. For the first time he had hope for the future, that maybe he'd found someone. He blasted the AC and the radio as he drove to his place, making it in record time because every light was mercifully green.

The moment they were inside the door, he kissed her with a passion rooted in newfound confidence. He tugged on the hem of her T-shirt so it came up and off. Cupped her breasts, ran his thumbs over the lace. His fingers traveled lower. "Checking for ticks. So far I don't see any."

Those tantalizing hands continued to caress her, sliding each bra strap down. He turned her so her back was to him, unhooked her bra. He lifted her hair, kissed the nape of her neck. Ran fingertips down her spine until he reached her waistband. "None here."

He turned her back around, put his fingers into her belt loops and pulled her to him. His lips crashed on hers. Then he undid her zipper, slid her shorts down. Dropped to his knees, caressed her legs. "Still none." He liked the way she gasped as his finger slid under the elastic of her panties. He rubbed her wetness, then pushed the fabric aside so he could taste. Her mewling cry was music to his ears, and he drank her until he pulled away. "I want to come inside you."

"Oh yes," she gasped and then her hands were on his shoulders guiding him up. She didn't even bother with his shirt, going straight to the button on his shorts. Joe's burned skin had been visible all day, but the moment of panic still came, and then ebbed. She'd never faltered. Never hesitated. Even now, she had her hand on his cock, one leg coming up around his waist.

They weren't in the bedroom. Heck, they hadn't even gotten out of the kitchen. Not his idea of romance, but she guided him into her heat, and he was lost. Her gaze locked on his as he began to move, and as he put one hand on the wall to thrust, her gaze never leaving his until she closed her eyes and made that noise deep in her throat that told him she was beginning to orgasm. "Yes," she told him, her eyes opening as she lifted her head to kiss him. "Oh yes."

Joe felt his own release power up until he let himself go deep inside. Then he cradled her. "I'll never look at this wall the same."

"Good," she told him, her breath beginning to slow.

"Because that was good. Really good."

He drew her further into his arms. "How about we get you cleaned up?"

"I am ready for the shower," she told him, the desire evident. "My turn to tick check."

He guided her into the bathroom, turned on the shower full force. He'd never showered with a woman before, but Taylor wasn't just anyone. Just like what had happened in the kitchen, he wanted this experience with her. He tested the water. Perfect. "Time to get wet."

Three hours later, Joe traced circles on her bare skin. "Okay, I want to see the photos."

She walked naked into the living room, returned with her camera to the bedroom. They lay together as she showed him the pictures.

"They're good," he approved.

"Thank you. I only need to make a few minor lighting corrections."

Joe admitted he looked great for a guy who didn't like being photographed. "I don't know if I'm comfortable letting anyone see them. I'm still not sure if I want to be in the burn survivors book. Especially with the calendar coming out too."

"Why don't you let me retouch them and you can decide? Personally, they're very sexy. I prefer these to Mr. September's shot. You're exposed. Vulnerable."

"No guy wants to be either," Joe pointed out. He moved his finger up her arm to her shoulder.

"More human. Women like to know the man beneath

the tough exterior. Like me with you. I definitely like you better than I did that first day."

"It's the Marino charm."

"It's more than that, and you and I both know it." She placed the camera safely onto the nightstand and inhaled. "I might be falling for you."

"Is that a bad thing?"

"It is if you don't think you're falling for me. That this is just sex."

Joe's gaze searched hers. "It's more than just sex."

Taylor exhaled. "Good. That makes me happy."

"I want to make you happy," Joe told her.

Taylor curved into him. He'd agreed to the photos. Doing the shoot had been a huge step. He'd done it because he trusted her. A warm feeling overtook her. Yes, this was more than sex.

He lowered his lips to her shoulder. "By the way," he told her between kisses, "before I forget, I'm working this weekend."

"On the fourth?" That was Friday.

"All of it. I'm picking up a shift for Parker on Sunday, so I'm going to do more than my normal forty-eight and pull some overtime. He and Susie are taking Winnie on a mini-vacation."

"A vacation sounds nice. I'm scheduled at Presley's. It's going to be busy with Fair St. Louis."

"So we wouldn't have seen each other much anyway."

"I'll be sad to miss the fireworks. I always liked seeing those."

"How about we create some of our own?"

She flipped over and reached for the part of him that was ready for her. Wondered if she'd ever get enough of him. "A very good idea."

***

Once the holiday hit, she didn't see Joe again until Monday, July 7, and then she saw him only briefly, for his brothers were all going fishing and camping for two days and he'd agreed to go with. She didn't mind. She was mostly wrapping up her photo shoots and, thanks to both Joe's mom and Virginia, she had a lot of work lined up.

Also, after he'd left, in a display of how small town St. Louis really was, her mom's friend's connection at *St. Louis Magazine* was none other than Ginger Redmond. When Ginger had realized who Taylor was after she had shot her family portraits, she had offered Taylor a staff job.

Taylor had a week to decide whether to accept, but she been on cloud nine ever since the offer and currently planned to say yes. While the pay wasn't much, it was decent, full-time work, with health insurance. Even better, she could keep doing freelance photography and quit Presley's.

She checked her phone as she waited in the conference room for the Wednesday afternoon appointment she'd scheduled with her professor, laughing at a text from Joe. He'd sent her a picture of his only catch—a pathetic tiny sunfish he'd thrown back into the stream.

"Taylor. Good to see you." Her professor shook her hand. Sat down. "Thanks for e-mailing these. I've had a chance to look through them."

"And?" She scooted to the edge of the chair.

"Congratulations. This is exactly what I wanted."

Taylor resisted the urge to jubilantly thrust fisted hands in the air. "Also"—and for the first time her professor really smiled—"I'm proud to tell you that five of your photos will be on display in our summer juried art show. While the deadline's passed, I contacted the director on your behalf and upon seeing your work, he made a special exception, something I've never seen him do. It's last minute, but the show's this Friday night at seven. I took the liberty of giving him the go-ahead. Your photos are being printed as we speak."

Taylor gasped. "This Friday?" Oh God. She hadn't expected this. She planned to show her professor her pictures, go home, and pop some bubbly. The photos she'd used, the ones Joe hadn't yet wanted her to show the general public even in his book, were about to go on display. "So I'm in the show."

Her professor nodded. "Yes. From seven to ten. You can be here?"

She'd have to change her Presley's shift but that was doable. Soon she'd be able to quit waitressing altogether. What was really important, though, was telling Joe. And praying he didn't believe she'd used him.

"Invite your family and friends. It's quite an honor. Congratulations, Taylor. After Friday night, your degree is complete. I have to run, but I'll see you at the gallery."

She sat there, stunned, the directions to the gallery in hand. A job offer. Her degree. Inclusion in the summer show. Perhaps Joe had been correct, for suddenly Lady Luck seemed to have entered Taylor's life. Maybe whatever cosmic bill she'd owed had been stamped "Paid in Full."

Except for the fact that she had to tell Joe. She wouldn't see him tonight as he wouldn't be back until after midnight, and he would start a twenty-four hour work shift tomorrow at seven a.m. He couldn't attend her show—so he wouldn't see the photos anyway.

They had planned to see each other all day Saturday, and then on Sunday she was taking his family's portraits. Tonight she'd just mention that her project was done and that she'd been included in the show. Saturday, she'd tell him everything. Also, Owen had stopped texting her, so she could tell him not to worry. She'd been right. Silence was golden, and ignoring Owen had been best.

***

Friday night Taylor wore the strapless peach Alice and Olivia dress she'd worn to Virginia's dinner party. As she stepped into the art gallery with her mother, she worked to calm her nerves. Around the room, people studied and discussed the pieces on display. A crowd stood in front of her set of five pictures, which included Joe's victory photo and the photo of him in the field.

"Beautiful work," her mother said as she wove her way

through the crowd. "Proud of you. Your dad would be too. I'm glad I'm here. I'd miss Bunco for this any day."

"Thanks." A tear misted in Taylor's eye, and she blinked it away. "I had a good subject."

A woman overheard her and turned to Taylor. "Are you the artist?"

"The photographer, yes," Taylor confirmed.

"Is your work for sale?"

Taylor shook her head, the updo not budging. "Oh, no. I couldn't part with these."

She handed Taylor her business card. "If you change your mind, call me."

Her mother stared at Taylor. "Did you hear her? She wanted to buy your work."

"I can't sell Joe, Mom."

Her mother studied the photographs, which had been printed 16 x 20, matted, and framed. "No, I guess not. I didn't realize he'd been burned."

"Yes," Taylor said, glad only one of those photos hung on the wall. Guilt crept in. She'd violated Joe's trust. Taking the path of least resistance didn't sit well.

"Hey, sorry we're late." Marci blew into the space. "Mrs. Krebs, this is Thad. Thad, Taylor and my second mom."

"Nice to meet you," Thad said. "Thanks for the invite."

"Glad you could make it." Taylor gave Marci a hug.

"You're my best friend," Marci said. "Even with twenty-four hours' notice, I wouldn't miss it. Just forgive us for not staying long. "

"That's right. You had the play."

"We still have time to make it as long as you don't mind we're just popping by."

Taylor shook her head. "Of course not."

"These are really great," Marci said. "I can see why you love him."

"I don't . . ." Taylor started to protest, then closed her mouth. Joe consumed her thoughts. Made her happy. She counted the minutes until she'd see him again. As conversation flowed around her, Taylor pulled herself back into the present. Saturday would come soon enough, and she had so much to share. *Please let him forgive me. Please let him understand.*

"Sorry we couldn't stay longer," Marci said as she gave Taylor a kiss on the cheek. "I'll talk to you tomorrow."

"You better," Taylor said, watching as Marci and Thad left. She turned back to her work, studying the expression on Joe's face, the one that hinted at his hidden depths.

"These are good. I always knew you'd do great work."

Taylor froze. She recognized that voice. *Owen.*

She turned slowly, seeing him standing next to her. Her photographer's eye still saw him as beautiful, but her heart and head knew what lurked underneath his Nordic god looks. Dread filled her. "What are you doing here?"

"We need to talk and you won't return my texts."

She folded her arms, refusing to be intimidated. "We have nothing to say."

Taylor's mother put a hand on her daughter's elbow.

"Perhaps you should hear him out."

Taylor whirled to face her mom. "You're the one who gave him my phone number?"

"Yes, but I didn't invite him here tonight. He stopped by the house earlier, and I mentioned that I was meeting you—Oh." Her mom's face fell. "Owen, you shouldn't have come here," Taylor's mom chastised.

"I'm desperate. Hear me out. Then I'll go," Owen pleaded. "Let me tell you what I told your mother. I'm sorry if I scared you again. I don't mean you any harm. Please."

Taylor, not wanting to create a scene, fumed, trapped. "Okay. Talk."

He shoved his hands into his dress pants pockets. Only a few inches taller, she stared at him eye to eye.

"I came to apologize."

Her lips puckered. "It's far too late for that."

His earnest expression didn't waver. "I know, but it's part of my program."

"What, are you doing Twelve Steps?"

He nodded. "Yes."

"Really?" She hadn't been expecting that answer. Had been sarcastic. She paused. Took a good, long, hard look.

"Making direct amends to people I've harmed is Step Nine." He pulled a chip out of his pocket. Held it out so she could see. "I've been sober over a year. Alcohol interferes with my bipolar medication. I also went through anger management classes."

She frowned. Couldn't quite believe. "I saw you at

Presley's. Your table ordered a bucket of beer."

"But I didn't drink any. I'm always the designated driver." He glanced around. More people were coming to view her photos. "Do you mind if we step away, just a little?"

"There's a bench over there." Taylor pointed to an alcove where she'd still be in view of her mom. "I do want to hear this," she told him. "But I think I need to sit down."

***

When Joe's cell phone buzzed around seven thirty, he was twelve hours away from the end of his shift, which so far had included four car accidents, three overdoses, two heart attacks, and a grease fire. The latter was the most recent call, and the reason he currently smelled like smoke. While the family would need a new kitchen, luckily no one had been injured.

Just off the truck, he stood in the bay and answered the call. "This is Joe."

"It's Marci."

"Hey." Joe's nerves went on high alert. "What's going on?"

"I was at Taylor's art show, and when I left I saw Owen."

"You mean the art show for her class?" He'd assumed when she'd told him about the show it was a class thing. Like everyone in her class shared a picture or something. It was public?

"Yes, that art show." Marci named the gallery, and Joe's frown deepened. "I saw Owen walking in when I was driving away. Her mom is with her, but I'm worried."

"She'll be okay, Marci. I'm on it."

"Thanks. I'm at the theater and the play's about to start. I'm on a date. Do you need me?"

"No. I've got it. Stay on your date." Joe hung up. Cursed. Loudly.

"You okay lieutenant?" Reid asked.

No, he wasn't okay. Far from it. He was trapped. The truck needed four guys. There was no way he could get to Taylor. He had to help her, but he was the senior officer on duty. He couldn't leave.

Not without a replacement.

"Give me a minute." He dialed Susie's number. She answered. "Hey. What's up?"

"Parker home?"

"Yes. He's putting Winnie to bed."

"I need him."

She must have heard the urgency in his voice, for Parker was immediately on the line. "Hey Joe. What's up?"

"I need you to cover for me." Joe said, mentally calculating that Parker lived less than five minutes away.

"Sure, no problem. When?"

"Right now," Joe told him. "I need you right now."

***

An hour later, Taylor remained on the bench talking

to Owen. She couldn't fathom everything he'd told her. Upon their breakup, he'd gone ballistic. "The restraining order was the wake-up call," he'd told her. "I lost it. But eventually I had to admit I was stalking you."

"You didn't attend the hearing. That's why the judge granted it."

"I refused to accept I was at fault. I blamed you. Hell, I blamed everyone for my problems and actions. Then one day I woke up drunk off my ass and wanted to kill myself. And I got help. Took two weeks off and checked into a clinic. It saved my life."

The medicine had made a difference, he'd told her. He'd also stopped drinking, which hadn't been easy. He'd changed jobs, giving himself a fresh start. Two years later, he'd begun really applying the Twelve Steps. "I want to marry Emily," he told her. "I love her. She knows my past, but she didn't live through it. She accepts me for me. She makes me happy. But I couldn't move on until I'd apologized to you. I did a number on you, and I'm sorry. I didn't mean to scare you again. I really had to convince your mom to give me your number."

"She probably should have mentioned it."

"I asked her not to; she agreed it was our business. Your mom is the type that gives someone a second chance."

"Yes, that she does," Taylor said. She'd talk with her misguided mother later. Despite the blindside, however, she understood her mother's reasoning. Her mom wanted Taylor to have closure, and now, after talking to Owen, an odd peace had settled over her. She'd never have to look behind her again. Owen had moved on. She had too. Her future was the man in the photograph—the man who had just walked in wearing turnout pants, suspenders, a blue T-shirt, and a layer of soot. A murmur raced through the crowd.

She rose to her feet, shocked. "Joe?"

"Taylor?" He strode over. Glared angrily at Owen, who'd risen shakily to his feet. She put her hand out, stopping Joe before he reached out and throttled her ex. "Marci called me."

Marci. Another meddler. Taylor wrapped her fingers around his arm, smelled the smoke that clung to him. He'd been fighting a fire. "I'm okay."

Taylor's mom joined the queue. Thrust out her hand. "You must be Joe. I'm Taylor's mom Deidre."

"Taylor, thank you for speaking with me." Owen tried to ease away.

"Don't move," Joe commanded. Owen froze.

"Owen came to apologize," Taylor told him. "He's doing Twelve Steps. It seems my mom gave him my number."

"And did you accept his apology?"

Taylor tried to diffuse Joe's tension. "I did. He's going to marry that girl you saw at Presley's."

Joe stared down Owen until the smaller man flinched and withered. "If you're done, get out. Don't ever bother Taylor again."

"Got it." As Owen backtracked, Taylor knew she'd never see him again. Her professor approached. "Is there a problem?"

"No, none," Taylor inserted quickly. Her hand still on Joe's arm, she could feel the rigidity radiating off him in waves.

"You're the guy in the photographs." Oblivious, her professor stuck his hand out but Joe didn't take it. "I've worked with Taylor for a year now and this is the best work I've ever seen her produce. I told her to capture your humanity. Your soul. She did just that. In fact, Taylor, I want to be the first to congratulate you. You've won."

"Won?"

"Yes. We'll announce it from the podium in five minutes, so don't go anywhere, but the thousand-dollar cash prize is yours. I couldn't be more pleased. I had to really push Taylor to take these photos, but you were the perfect subject," he told Joe. "So raw and emotional. Perfect."

He moved away. Joe looked at Taylor. Then he trailed his gaze and saw the photographs on the far wall.

Freeing himself, boots that left a trail of grit walked over to where Taylor's work hung. The crowd parted like the Red Sea so the firefighter could see his photos.

She followed him. Drew abreast. "Do you want to explain this?" he bit out.

"I didn't know my professor was going to submit them or hang them up. I found out Wednesday afternoon."

The fact Wednesday was days ago hung in the air.

"So I'm your project. Did you ever plan on telling me?" The words were quiet, deadly, and meant for her ears only.

"Yes. Tomorrow."

He said nothing for the longest minute of her life. Then, the gallery director tapped his champagne flute and everyone grew quiet. "Ladies and gentlemen, the winner of tonight's juried prize and the cash prize of a thousand dollars goes to Taylor Krebs for her work 'Firefighter Expose.'"

Around Taylor applause erupted. But Joe stood there, saying nothing. Instead of celebrating, she wanted to drop through the floor.

"Parker's covering. He needs to get home. I have to get back. Glad I could help you win some money. "

"Joe," she protested in vain, for he strode out without another word, the turnout pants making a swishing noise, grit falling in his wake.

"Taylor, come on up," the director called, all smiles. She walked on autopilot, took the check that weeks ago would have meant so much. Now victory seemed hollow. She smiled for the requisite photos. Accepted endless congratulations.

Inside her heart was breaking.

"It'll be fine." Her mother patted her on the arm after Taylor finished her winner's duties.

Inside Taylor's stomach felt like lead. "You don't understand. He's a proud man. He never wanted me to expose him publicly like this. I figured what he wouldn't know wouldn't hurt him, and I'd tell him after the fact. I screwed this all up. I made a huge mistake. I've ruined everything."

"He'll get over it," her mother said with complete confidence.

Taylor whirled on her. "How do you know?"

"Because he loves you. Why else would he be here, ready to defend you?"

Taylor blinked. Joe had called Parker. Left the firehouse in the midst of his shift. For her. Who knew what that had cost him?

"I have to go after him."

"Taylor, there you are," her professor called. "I want you to meet someone,"

Her mom shook her head. "You have to finish here. There's nothing you can do until you see him again. Time has a way of working these things out."

"He's not going to want to see me again." That Taylor knew for certain. "I have to do something." She reached into her wristlet, withdrew her phone, and stepped into a corner. She dialed a number.

Susie picked up on the first ring. "Hey. What's up?"

"I really screwed up." Taylor quickly filled her in.

But instead of being upset, Susie laughed. "I wish I could have seen his face. About time he gets over his fear of people knowing the real Joe that all of us love so fiercely."

"This is serious," Taylor hissed, wishing she could shout her frustration. Susie wasn't helping.

Susie got herself under control. "Oh Taylor, it is serious. You do love him, don't you?"

"Yes. Without a shred of doubt."

"Then we've got your back. We've all been waiting for Joe to meet his match, and he finally has in you."

"He's proud. He's not going to want—"

Susie interrupted. "You called me for advice, didn't you? Not just to confess, blather and wallow?"

Taylor moved deeper into the alcove. Returned to the bench. "I love him," she admitted again. "So yes. I need advice. I don't want to lose him."

"Good." Susie seemed pleased. "Now here's exactly what you're going to do."

Chapter Thirteen

The rest of Joe's shift had been relatively quiet, or at least nothing major, which was good because he'd been on a tear the rest of the night. Even his crew gave him a wide berth.

He'd been an idiot. He knew he shouldn't have trusted her. He'd never felt so betrayed—this was why he'd always kept women at a distance. Yet he'd let Taylor in, and she'd used him. All those eyes on his photographs. On him—all of them staring at what he chose to keep hidden from the world.

So intent on those thoughts, he almost missed seeing Taylor's car parked in the spot next to his. A quick glance told him she wasn't in it. He entered his apartment building, where he found her sitting with her knees up to her chest on the stairs outside his door. "How long have you been there?"

"About ten minutes. Susie told me when you'd be home."

Damn his sister. He looked at Taylor and waited for

the rage to come. But it didn't, he wanted to pull her close and kiss her breathless, instead he schooled his expression and said, "I'm leaving again, you should go."

She stood and blocked his path. "I know I am the last person you want to see, and I swore I would never act like Owen, who literally stalked me. But you and I made a promise to be honest with each other, so that's what I am going to do."

"Honesty would have been telling me my photographs were hanging in a public art gallery. You won money by exposing me."

"Yes, I did, and I'm sorry. I thought only my professor was going to see the pictures. Then when I get to my meeting, he tells me they are already entered in the show and at that point there was nothing I could do. You were out of town. I figured I'd tell you later. My mistake. My misstep and one I'll live with for the rest of my days. But I'm proud of my work. I'm proud of you."

He stared at her, his expression unreadable. "We have nothing more to say to each other."

She stomped her foot, a childish gesture that she regretted immediately. But how to get through to him? "Before last night, you were falling in love with me."

"What does it matter? If I was, I don't feel anything anymore." Joe lied. He knew it. So did she.

"Like hell. Stop being so damn stubborn. You're just like me. A stubborn fool. Well, guess what, I love you. And I didn't hang you on a wall because I'm using you. We can take the money and donate it in your name to the

BackStoppers for all I care." She jutted her chin forward. "Seriously. I'm proud of who you are, and of the man you've become. Damn, I don't believe I'm even going to say this, but if Owen could figure out that he was bipolar and he needed to help himself, then maybe the great Joe Marino could, just once, figure out how to love himself. I love you, and it would be a shame for you to you throw us away because you're still feeling guilty for a mistake you made when you were twelve."

Her chest heaved. She took a flash drive from the purse on her shoulder and thrust it at him. "See yourself as I see you. See that you deserve to be loved, and stop being a stupid martyr. We're all tired of it." She gasped for breath.

Pride and stubbornness. His worst flaws. His voice almost didn't work, and when it did, he simply said, "You through?"

"Yes." Her lower lip quivered and she sunk her teeth into it.

He'd hurt her, and doing so didn't make him feel better. Actually, he felt lower than low. Head high, she began to walk past him. "I will see you tomorrow. Let's just get through this last shoot, and you and I can go our separate ways if that's what you want." With that parting shot, she strode off.

Joe stood there, the flash drive dangling in his fingers. He resisted the urge to toss it in the trash. Her words replayed in his head as the earlier anger he felt returned.

He didn't have a martyr complex.

The door across the hall creaked open, and his sister

Elaina poked her head out.

"Did you hear all that?" he snapped.

"Hard not to," she replied, the door creaking open further. "You sure she's not Italian? She sure put you in your place."

"You agree with her?"

Elaina shrugged. "You are pretty damn stubborn. It gets annoying sometimes. We're all adults now. No need be the big brother all the time. . . . And she loves you." Elaina shook her head. "Never believed that would happen, and you'd be foolish to throw that away because clearly you love her if you went to save her last night."

"And everyone already knows about that?"

She nodded. "News in this family travels fast. I'm sure Nana knows by now too. You know Nana adored her."

And Nana would want to smack him for his bad behavior. Joe threw his hands up. "So you think I should go after her?"

Elaina moved her long braid to the opposite shoulder. "I'm not a love guru. She said she'd see you tomorrow."

"We were supposed to spend today together. The family photos are tomorrow."

"So maybe that's what you meant. Well, you'll see her then."

The main door opened downstairs. Joe's heart jumped. Maybe she'd returned. But as a familiar figure appeared on the landing, Joe realized he'd been mistaken.

"Lieutenant," Reid said, edging a bit toward the wall. "Long time no see. Thought you'd be at the gym by now."

Joe gazed at his sister, who arched her eyebrows in silent challenge as she ushered Reid inside and out of sight. "We're spending the day at the Botanical Garden. You are officially on your own. And if you do anything to Reid, you deal with me. I like him. A lot. And he feels the same. Please do not screw anything else up."

With that, she shut her apartment door in Joe's face.

Joe stood on the landing, his entire world completely upside down. His sister was dating Reid. How long had that been going on? How long had they kept it from him?

But even that revelation didn't undo the bombshells Taylor had leveled on him. She'd shredded him to the core. Hurt his ego. Compared him to Owen.

That had been a low blow, one he'd deserved.

He inserted his key and dealt with Brutus who wanted his daily kibble. She'd also said she loved him. Thrown her declaration at his face. He probably deserved that too.

He sat at his kitchen table, let the events of the past twenty-four hours wash over him.

She loved him. Really loved him. He took the flash drive, pushed it into his laptop, and found the images she'd taken of him. He saw the entire applied photography project, not just the five that had hung on the wall.

She'd captured him, peeling back layers to peer into his soul. She really saw him, he realized. She loved him, burns and guilt be damned.

And as he realized she'd been right all along, and that he'd been a worthless jerk, Joe let the floodgates open.

For the first time since he'd seen the burns all over his

sister's arms and legs, felt the pain of his own seared skin as he carried her through the flames, he broke down and cried.

He cried until he'd worn himself out, until Brutus was in his face yowling with worry, until he'd purged himself of the remorse that he'd carried long after everyone else had shed their own.

He loved Taylor. She was different, and he was worthy of her love.

He stood, patted Brutus to let him know it was okay, then did what he did best. He was a man who never shied away from a challenge.

He got to work.

***

The immediate Marino clan, including Nana, numbered eighteen. Add in Marvin's brother and a bunch of cousins, and Taylor jostled give or take forty people for the family photo.

To make sure everyone would be visible, she and Judy had chosen the ball field bleachers at a local park. With the open ground behind them, the risers would work perfectly.

Taylor set up her tripod, adjusted the lens, and began to direct people.

A small crowd of onlookers had set up some lawn chairs—she weren't quite sure who they were, although one guy looked somewhat familiar. He kept talking to Elaina, but Taylor couldn't place him.

She checked the light. Checked the battery. Group photos were hard. Something always happened to make the photo useless. As the shutter snapped, someone would always have his eyes closed. Or someone would have a goofy smile. Another would be looking anywhere but at the camera. And people always kept touching their hair, even after she'd told them to put their hands in their lap if seated, or at their sides if standing.

Currently, the holdup was that Joe and Susie were missing. Parker had arrived with Winnie, who was having a hard time staying out of the dirt. She'd already grabbed two handfuls from the dugout and thrown it into the air. Parker was currently trying to dust off her dress.

The crowd on the bleachers grew slightly restless. At least they'd all followed her instructions to wear a similar color. The group all wore various shades of blue, making them somewhat color-coordinated.

"Ah, here comes Joe," his mother called.

Taylor's heart leapt into her throat as he approached wearing a long-sleeve blue shirt and darker blue dress pants. His sunglasses hid his beautiful eyes, and she noticed he'd cut his hair. She'd thought the slightly longer locks looked sexy, but the shorter length only heightened his appeal.

A cheer came from the mostly male onlookers, who raised various soda cans in salute. "About time. Let's get on with this show."

"Look at that sexy hair cut!"

"Who knew you'd clean up so well?"

Who were those people? Taylor tore her gaze away as Joe and Susie stepped onto the bleachers and into their assigned positions. Given Nana's age, Judy had wanted the family to sit for the photos.

Taylor gave everyone final directions, stood on the wooden stepladder she'd brought so the camera could be high up, and placed her eye to the viewfinder. Everyone was in the shot. "Okay everyone. Big smiles. One . . . two . . . three—"

"Stop!"

She jerked her head up. On the end, Joe was standing and climbing down the bleachers, which rattled with each step. "This isn't going to work. Let me see."

He approached the camera. Tall enough, he simply looked through the viewfinder without using the stepladder. "Nope. If we shoot this now we'll have to redo it later. I even cut my hair for this. Like it?"

Oh she did, but she bristled. Wouldn't give him the satisfaction. She'd fretted the entire day after she'd left him. Not one word. Not one text. Even Susie hadn't answered her calls. Marci, out with Thad who seemed to really like her even if she wasn't "of his class," had also been unavailable.

The sun was getting higher in the sky, the July day starting to get hot. "We need to get this done. Everyone's face is visible. They are all perfect."

"No, it's still wrong."

"Look again. You're the one who's wrong," she insisted. "I'm the photographer, remember?"

"How could I forget? You are a damn good one, as I could see for myself when I looked at the flash drive. But we're missing someone."

There were around forty people on the bleachers, the rest on the sidelines, all avidly watching the conversation. Taylor's nerves frayed. "Fine. Who are we waiting for?"

"You."

He'd taken off his sunglasses and smiled at her. "Can't have a photo if we're only going to have to retake it."

"I'm not a part of your family. Why would you need to retake it?"

He sighed. Reached into his pocket for something small and shiny. "Because if you love me, really, really love me like you insisted yesterday, you're going to marry me and be part of this family because I love you too. And I can't live without you. And I'm praying you'll forgive me for being a big jerk. A cad."

The word caught her attention as much as the ring he held out. A diamond glittered. "It was Nana's engagement ring. Goes to the oldest grandson. That's me." He gestured to the crowd. "Ignore them. They're just jealous."

She didn't even glance at the bleachers, her entire focus on Joe. His gaze held hers. "I know I can be an ass, but as Elaina pointed out yesterday, you know how to handle me. I want to grow old with you. What do you say?"

He dropped onto one knee, which immediately got a little dusty. "With my whole family as witnesses, I love you. You going to marry me?"

He held up the ring, which glittered in the morning

sun. She placed her hand on her mouth and burst into tears.

"You're supposed to say yes," someone called.

"Put on my lucky ring and marry my boy," Nana called.

"Yes!" Taylor shouted, finding her voice. "Yes."

Everyone clapped, including the onlookers. Whoever they were, they added cheers and whistles. "Ignore them," Joe told her, standing up. "That's my crew. You can put them into their place too. They'll deserve it.'

"Kiss the girl," one of them shouted.

"See? Getting there!" Joe shouted and Taylor laughed as he put the most gorgeous antique ring on her finger and twirled her around.

Marci and her mother appeared from somewhere, and there were hugs all around until Judy called from the bleachers. "Can we take this photo now? I want a hug too and we've been forbidden to move until it's done."

"And I'm hot," Nana called. "Get on in here, Taylor."

"Yes," Taylor called back, laughing. "Let's do this thing."

So Taylor looked through the viewfinder, and told Marci to get on the stepladder.

"I don't know what I'm doing," Marci protested.

"You count to three and press the button. I've set it up. Anyone can do it. Take at least three pictures, and then I'll come check."

"Okay, I'll try. No guarantees." Marci gazed through the viewfinder as Joe held Taylor's hand and led her to their spot on the bleachers. Susie sat to Taylor's left.

"Welcome to the family," she said, giving Taylor's hand a squeeze.

Marci leaned back, looked at everyone. "Okay. Smile. Hands down in your laps. Hey, that means you." She stared them down. "Perfect. Hold that."

Joe grabbed Taylor's hand. Held it out of sight.

"Ready?" Marci called. "Say cheese on one, two, three."

"Cheese!" everyone shouted, and as the shutter opened and closed. Taylor added her wide, happy smile next to the grin of the man she loved, and the camera froze their love for all eternity—as instead of looking at the camera, they were looking into each other's eyes.

Sneak Peek

Mr. December

Chapter One

"Up on the rooftop, reindeer paws . . ."

Or was it "pause"? As the chorus of impromptu Christmas caroling began—and it wasn't even Thanksgiving—Jack Donovan tugged at the annoying starched edge of his white shirt collar. Tuxedos were for proms and weddings—tonight was neither. He skirted the edge of the Chase Park Plaza's Khorassan Ballroom—supposedly the best in St. Louis—ignoring the two well-heeled women who gave him pointed looks before blushing and giggling.

Jack adjusted his black bow tie, wishing he could remove the required dress-code noose. While he really didn't have anywhere else to be, this was so not his scene. If the floor opened and swallowed him whole, he wouldn't mind. Maybe then he could also ditch the rented jacket that tightened every time he crossed his arms.

He eased into a corner, ensuring he was clear of the mistletoe sprigs hanging strategically between dangling strands of soft, tiny, white Christmas lights. He sipped from the brown long-necked bottle he'd been carrying for most of the evening, the King of Beers now lukewarm.

Celebratory cheers erupted as the carol reached its crescendo, and then the band resumed, much to Jack's relief. Christmas started earlier and earlier every year. Case in point, it was only seven days into November and some decorator had gone crazy with the holiday decorations: the ballroom was littered with poinsettias, miniature Christmas trees, silvery stars, glittery snowmen, and that damn mistletoe he'd been dodging all night.

He moved deeper into the shadows, edging around one of the almost life-size cutouts of the single men featured in the first Sexy Public Servants of St. Louis Charity Calendar. He'd known Joe Marino, firefighter and Mr. September, since Catholic youth soccer when they'd faced each other twice in the championship round. Now both were the faces of local charities, but while Joe seemed to relish the growing crowd of women, Jack wasn't thrilled with his sudden fame as Mr. December.

Unlike Joe, who'd at least gotten to wear turnout gear suspenders, pants, and coat in his photo, Jack wore only a Santa hat and low-rise jeans in his. Across the room a crowd of women added him to their Instagram accounts by surrounding and posing with the nearly naked cardboard version of Jack in all his holiday glory. Did one woman just paw his cardboard chest? Jack rolled his eyes heavenward. Great. More ammunition for his mother, the South Side's expert matchmaker. He loved his mother, but lately she had been harping on how he needed to find his soul mate, settle down, and start a family. She'd also been tossing women at him right and left. As the holiday season approached, she'd redoubled her efforts. Jack so far had avoided Susie Crenshaw, Alice Foster, and Laura Sims—who were all on his mom's current list of potential dates. All three had made a beeline for him earlier, clearly preprogramed to seek him out. As he'd signed Susie's calendar, she had slipped him her phone number.

Jack dangled the beer bottle between his fingertips and wished he could leave. What the hell had he been thinking, agreeing to all this? Oh yeah, his lieutenant had insisted, and one did not cross Lt. Steven Jones. Besides, Jack had been told, the calendar needed a cop, and as Jack was the face of the six-month-old St. Louis Police Department's Animal Cruelty Task Force, saying no hadn't been an option.

The publicity would be good exposure, he'd been assured. Considering the state of undress in Mr. December's photo, he'd been exposed all right. Thankfully, one-twelfth of the proceeds went to pet charities he'd been able to personally select so, at least some good would come out of his embarrassment. Even so, he couldn't help but grimace as some woman across the room tweaked his one-dimensional nipple and took a selfie; he prayed it was only a Snapchat that faded after a few seconds. As it was, his damn photo was already up on Google images, and two days ago the guys at the precinct had decorated his locker with hundreds of overlapping, baseball-card-size copies. It had taken a full twenty minutes to peel off the tape slivers.

A tall brunette caught his attention as she wove through the crowd, a long expanse of leg sliding through the thigh-high slit in her red dress. He didn't realize he was staring until she stood directly in front of him and held out her hand. "Hi," she said, her voice creating a shiver of awareness he hadn't felt in years. "You must be Jack. I'm Kat."

Damn. Talk about being caught off guard. He smiled automatically, as he'd been doing all night. "Hi."

Her fingers warmed under his, and he instinctively held on a second too long before letting go. Odd. "So someone"—she looked over her shoulder as if searching for that person—"told me you're the first member of the mayor's new task force."

"It says that in the calendar, yes."

Susie Crenshaw walked past, head swiveling as she searched for someone; Jack sank deeper into the shadows, closer to the emergency exit doors.

Kat noticed, and moved helpfully to block him. "Ex?"

Jack shook his head. "Nothing like that."

"Ah." Mirth lifted perfect lips, and her brown eyes twinkled. "One of your groupies. I saw how they fawned over you. Don't worry. You're safe with me."

Since his interest in the opposite sex had chosen this moment to reemerge, he wasn't so sure anyone was safe. That beautiful mouth begged to be kissed. He searched for a benign topic, then said the first thing that came to mind. "Did you buy a calendar? Did I already sign it?" He'd signed hundreds earlier during the group autograph session.

Although surely he would have remembered her. Those succulent red lips—lips that matched the color of her sleeveless velvet dress—wrapped around the edge of her champagne flute, and as she swallowed, Jack's underused libido flared to life. Brown hair up in a knot revealed a creamy white neck perfect for planting kisses on, and he longed to just that. He hardened.

"Ten of them actually and no, I'm good."

His eyebrows arched. Lost in trying to calm his lower half, had he heard her correctly? "You bought ten?"

She laughed, a light melodic sound that he wouldn't mind hearing over and over again. "It's for charity, and I'll give them to my staff."

She fingered the gold chain at her neck, and his gaze traced the filament down to where the jewelry dipped into the V of breasts caressed by hugging velvet. But with his mom's "Eyes up, Buster" admonition ingrained in his head since puberty, he focused on her face—and found brown eyes a man could drown in as he counted each little gold speck. And when those long brown lashes fluttered down . . . He swore his heart skipped.

Those red lips puckered humorously as she added, "Oh, and I can't forget a calendar for my grandmother, who's in a nursing home and says she's never too old to look. I'm sure she'll like your . . . Santa hat."

"And you?" The words popped out of his mouth, his genuine interest surprising him. He could practically hear his mother shout "Saints be praised!" For the past two years, ever since Julie ended their five-year relationship because of his commitment phobia, he'd felt not a flicker of interest. "How's your Christmas spirit?"

A rosy flush that matched her dress spread over her pale skin, momentarily distracting him. If the band played, he didn't hear it. Time seemed to freeze, if only for a second. "So?" he teased.

She shifted her weight, the revealing slit showcasing a long expanse of creamy mile-high leg his fingers itched to caress. Her mouth wrapped around the flute edge, and she took another long sip before replying. Underneath his jacket, Jack started to sweat. *Had someone turned up the heat?* "Well, everyone knows December is my favorite month. I love Christmas and everything that comes with it. . . ."

"Including Santa hats?"

"Maybe. I've been known to wear one or two when the occasion warranted."

That beautiful laugh trilled again, and those lashes fluttered down. Bright red painted nails toyed with her necklace, the color a seductive contrast against her pale skin. Desire to see her wearing nothing but heels and his hat made Jack lose his train of thought. Two years of nothing, not one iota or flicker of interest in the opposite sex, and suddenly—

"Jack! There you are!"

Jack winced at the familiar voice. Not only was Virginia Edwards Barker a doppelganger for a tad younger

Betty White, but the seventy-something socialite could rival Jack's grandmother in determination and grit in getting her way. She'd been bossing the calendar men around all evening.

"Looks like I'm needed," Jack said as the head of the charity calendar committee made a beeline for him. "Not that I wasn't enjoying this."

"Can we talk later?" Kat asked. Her fingers touched his arm. "I love animals. I'd like to get more involved and . . ."

Even through two layers of clothing he felt the searing of her touch, as if she'd branded his skin. Nerves short-circuited; his brain registered only the word *involved*. How many women tonight had asked him, "Are you involved with anyone? Would you like to be?" How many phone numbers had been thrust at him? He stepped backward, that distasteful word like a bucket of ice-cold water.

"Finally!" Virginia caught her breath and smoothed her taffeta gown. "It's taken me five minutes to find you. We're going to do a group photo for the paper. Did you forget?"

He never forgot anything, and his sharp mind was one reason he'd become a detective. He saw clues others missed and could recall them long after the fact. However, for a man who loved being in control, he had lost track of time and hated the idea of yet another picture. At least this time he'd be clothed. Jack faced Kat, those full red lips begging to be kissed, his emotions and memory a rare jumble. Maybe he had heard her wrong?

"Jack . . ." Virginia prompted.

"Kat—" he began, but before he finished, Virginia gave a delighted, joyous little clap. "Jack! Look up."

She pointed and Jack's gaze automatically followed, registering the mistletoe he'd been avoiding all night, especially after Alice Foster almost caught him underneath. Kat's deep brown eyes widened and her lush, inviting mouth formed a shocked O.

"Kiss, dear, it's tradition," Virginia commanded. She gave Kat a helpful push, and Jack drew her into an embrace, steadying her. His fingers sizzled as they touched her bare forearms. Then she wobbled on her stilettos and fell against his chest as a startled breath burst forth. His heart raced, and as need pulsed through him, he knew he had to taste her lips. Just one quick taste to get it out of his system . . .

The kiss lasted mere seconds, but even that one feathery touch sent a shockwave of desire to his already tight pants. He stepped back, having only a moment to register Kat's dazed expression before Virginia grabbed his arm and propelled him onward. "Find him after the photo, hon," she said. "You can reconnect then."

However, later, when Jack—despite his earlier intentions to escape—went to find Kat, she was gone.

Acknowledgments

To Jennifer Stevenson and Elizabeth Ann West, for without them this version of the book would not be possible. Your friendship means the world to me. And to Michael Eisenbeis, who graciously told me all about firefighting. You rock.

About the Author

Describing herself as a woman who does way too much and never wants to stop, Michele Dunaway is a bestselling author and award-winning high school English teacher. Proud mother of two daughters, Michele is an avid pet lover who shares her home with far too many rescued cats, who of course completely rule the roost.